LAURA'S SECRET

anny's face was filled with curiosity. As Laura stepped out of the car, she took a deep breath hoping she could relieve the pressure that had mounted due to this inevitable talk. Laura lifted herself up on a concrete table and prepared herself to speak. She tossed her hair back and pulled her blouse away from her stomach.

"Danny, I don't know how to tell you this," she began. "It's been two-and-a-half months, and we're about to finish our junior year. I don't know how this happened," she began to speak nervously and quickly. "Well, I know how it happened; but I can't believe it happened to me, to us. I had so many plans for the future."

Danny put his hands on Laura's shoulder, "Slow down, what are you trying to tell me?"

"Danny, I've ruined your life and mine," she continued with tears running down her face.

LAURA'S

SECRET

CHUSMA HOUSE

CHUSMA HOUSE PUBLICATIONS

Copyright © 1997 by Irma Garcia

Published by Chusma House Publications
P.O. Box 467, San José, CA 95103-0467

ISBN: 0-9624536-8-4

Library of Congress Catalog Card Number: 97-65875

First Printing

Patson's Press, Sunnyvale, California

Printed in Aztlán

Cover Illustration/Production
Hiram Duran Alvarez

Edited by
Margarita Maestas-Flores

CHAPTERS

ONE
5

TWO
21

THREE
25

FOUR
29

FIVE
41

SIX
59

SEVEN
63

EIGHT
73

NINE
79

TEN
87

ELEVEN
89

TWELVE
97

THIRTEEN
101

FOURTEEN
109

FIFTEEN
113

SIXTEEN
127

SEVENTEEN
147

EIGHTEEN
159

NINETEEN
163

TWENTY
171

TWENTY-ONE
175

TWENTY-TWO
181

TWENTY-THREE
189

CHAPTER ONE

*T*he sun whipped mercilessly across the dry Texas earth, reaching a scorching 102 degrees. Laura Garza, Anna Guzmán, and Thelma Muñoz seemed oblivious to the hot Texas sun. Their soft, brown skins flicked with tones of golden yellow gave images of healthy children. They'd accepted the summers that felt as if they were inside a hot stove. They enjoyed Laura's backyard with its two huge trees, entwined into one another, shrouding the backyard with cool shade. This gave refuge from the hot and humid afternoons.

Anna's mom had skillfully French braided her brown hair, hair that gleamed with golden highlights. It seemed as if she'd been kissed by the sun. Thelma's hair was short and just to the bottom of her ear lobe. It was cut this way, Mrs. Muñoz said, because of the many siblings Thelma had. This left more time for chores and less for combing. Her cropped, black, shiny hair enhanced her hazel eyes. Her tall, lanky body looked malnourished. Thelma's mom tried diligently to stuff her with tonics to help her put on weight. Nothing ever seemed to work.

Thelma didn't seem to mind being the oldest of eight siblings. When the situation got out of hand with her brothers and sisters and her patience was low, there was nowhere to seek refuge in the small wooden home. She would simply grab a library book she'd checked out in school and walk across the street to a citrus grove. There, in her own enchanted and over-expanded imagination, she had turned a grapefruit tree into her own personal room. With the help of her oldest brother Beto they had cleaned out the brush from under the tree and found an old cloth to use as the floor. She had her very own place to call her own. She had been able to keep old books passed on to her by her teachers. To her, it was a magical library. It was her very own secret hiding place known only to Beto and her.

There was deep trust and respect between Thelma and Beto. He was the only one who could visit there; and he, at times, sat and read books with Thelma.

She would fall into a dream of her own, far away from home. It was as if the earth had opened up for a moment and swallowed her, taking her to places she'd never been.

Today Thelma's parents had given her special permission to go to Laura's house for the weekend.

Thelma and Laura had met at school. Thelma was bussed from her neighborhood to a school that met the needs of advanced children. It was there, in Mrs. González's second-grade classroom, that their friendship began. The girls met and became instant best friends.

Laura came hopping back from inside her house. "I found a sheet. Mom said we could use it to sit on." With Thelma's help, Laura spread the sheet out on the grass.

"There, that's better," said Anna as she slapped her neck softly to kill a bug. She bent down and picked up a fallen leaf and wiped the dead bug from her hand.

"Okay, who's first?" asked Laura anxiously, holding the monopoly game to her chest.

"I am. I'll be first!" yelled Anna. "This time, I promise not to get angry if I go bankrupt or get put in jail," said Anna with a grin.

"Yeah, it's only a game anyway," said Laura. They all sat Indian style and chose their charms. They appointed Thelma as the banker. Laura grabbed the bun her mom had made of her thick, brown hair. She readjusted a hairpin then clapped her hands twice. "Okay, let's play."

Thelma wiped the sweat from her forehead. The girls proceeded to immerse themselves in the game.

Laura rolled the dice. "Three," she said as she counted and moved her charm. "I landed on your property, Anna."

Anna threw her hands up. "Yes, New York Avenue." Anna looked up toward the sky dreamily, "I can't wait until I'm all grown up. Yes, I know one day...." Anna took the sandal off her foot, grabbed it like a microphone, and began to sing into the shoe as she leaned toward the center of the group and continued her singing, "Yeah, hmmm...hmmm...hmmm..., small-town girl, don't know it all."

Thelma and Laura joined in. "Yeah, yeah, one day we'll have it all. We are the small town girls! Oh yeah!" they sang together.

When she finished singing, Anna accidently put her hand on the game board, causing it to fold and bringing an end to the game. No one seemed to mind. She stood up and took a few steps back to get some speed and to prepare for her grand finale, a round off, followed by four consecutive flip-flops. This act, so gracefully executed, was the result of the countless hours and years Anna practiced gymnastics. Anna's final landing was a Chinese split in which her pointed toes and elegant hand gestures demonstrated her ballet training. When Anna rose from her split, a sudden gust of wind seemed to pass through her. She lost her balance and felt dizzy.

"Are you okay, Anna?" questioned Laura.

"Sure. That's funny, I could have sworn the wind hugged me."

Laura and Thelma looked dumbfounded at each other but made no comment. It was no secret that Anna loved the spotlight. She had already made plans to try out for the cheerleading squad next year, as the girls entered junior high school the coming spring. Laura and Thelma continued pursuing their talents in English, writing, and math U.I.L. competitions and boasted every time they won a first-place ribbon or first-place trophy. Anna could hardly wait to take drama. She had gone to U.I.L. plays with her older sister Dolores. Dolores had won many trophies in acting. Anna was sure she'd do the same; and since her sister could teach her the ropes, there would be no stopping her. They would be famous actresses together even though Dolores was much older.

The girls continued the conversation as they entered Laura's house and walked into her bedroom.

"You know what I really want to be?" asked Laura, as she closed the door to her bedroom.

Anna plopped on Laura's bed while Thelma leaned her back against the dresser.

"Mom's taken me with her to work a few times and ...."

"You want to be a nurse like your mom?" interrupted Thelma.

"Hold on, silly dweeb. I saw this doctor while mom was busy with a patient. I left the nurses' station and followed him."

As the girls listened closely, Laura continued. "He went to the emergency room. You could hear the ambulance in the background and a lot of commotion. No one seemed to pay much attention to me, so I watched from behind a curtain. The ambulance people rushed in and were talking to the doctor. The patient was a little boy about eight. Apparently a dog had attacked him. His head was bleeding badly."

Anna frowned with disgust.

"Did you gross out?"

"No, I didn't."

Thelma crossed her arms.

"How old were you then, Laura?"

"Hmmm...I must have been about six. Maybe seven," answered Laura. Anna rolled over on the bed with her hands on her face. "What did you do then? I would have probably vomited."

"You know, that's just the thing. I watched as the doctor sewed his skull back together. I remember his ear had been torn, and the doctor also took care of that. I must have been so impressed, but you know what was even most impressive?"

Anna's eyes grew large, waiting for the words that came out of Laura's mouth to be gruesome.

"The doctor was a woman."

"She was a woman?" Anna's eyes dropped with disappointment. "That's it? You want to be a doctor and pull out guts? Is that it?" remarked Anna. She grabbed Laura and began pinching and tickling her stomach.

Laura giggled, "Stop, silly, what are you doing?" Laura sat up on the bed and whipped her hair over her shoulder. "Anna, you're so silly," she said as she pushed Anna away.

"Well, since we're talking about what we want to be when we grow up, I don't suppose you all could guess what I'd like to be?" asked Anna.

Thelma put her hands to her head, pretending to think hard. "Let me guess, an actress," she said mockingly.

"Yes, you are correct,"

Laura jumped on the bed. "You've told us before you dweeb. Now, Thelma, dear sweet Thelma, that leaves only you."

Thelma responded, "Oh, I don't know. I love math, I love English, and I love science. Whatever it is, I hope I'll be very good at it."

Anna stood by Thelma and put her hand on Thelma's hand. "Come on, you can tell us."

"I don't really know. I'd like to be a lawyer, but then I'd like to be a scientist. Maybe I'll be an English teacher. I'll tell you in a few more years."

As the girls continued chatting into the evening, the telephone rang. Thelma was sure it would be her parents telling Laura's mother, Mrs. Garza, to drive her home.

Mrs. Garza cautiously entered the room. Laura said, "Yes, Mom, Thelma's going home."

"Who is?" asked Mrs. Garza, with a far-away look in her eyes.

"Thelma's mom. Wasn't that her on the phone?"

Mrs. Garza put her hands to her mouth. "I'm sorry. I forgot to tell you Mr. Muñoz called a few hours ago when you were outside. He asked if you could spend the night. They are going to México to visit your uncle Manuel and are going to spend the night in Reynosa. They didn't want to cut your day short. They know how much you enjoy coming to visit Laura."

"Hurray!" yelled the girls in excitement, almost in unison.

"I'll call my parents, too, and ask them if I can spend the night. We'll make it a slumber party," declared Anna.

The girls' faces shined brightly as if they'd all been awarded with trophies.

"Anna."

"Yes, ma'am."

"That call was for you."

"What is it? Did someone die? You look scared." Instantly tears began to run down Mrs. Garza's face.

"It was your father who just telephoned." Her voice grew insecure. Instantly the girls froze. They sensed something was wrong.

"Mom, what is it?" asked Laura. Anna walked directly

up to Mrs. Garza.

"Is my mom okay?" questioned Anna.

"Mi hija, I'll drive you home. There has been an accident, a car accident."

Anna's body felt as if it would be ill. She sat on the bed feeling faint.

"They'll tell you when you get home."

"I need to know now, please."

There's been an accident. Your mom is in stable condition. She's all right."

Laura embraced Anna. "It's going to be all right."

Anna looked over Laura's shoulder. "There's more, Mrs. Garza, tell me."

"Your brother Joey broke his legs, but he's going to be okay."

"Can you take me to the hospital? My sister will probably be there waiting for me."

Mrs. Guzmán let out a cry of sorrow.

"Can you take me to the hospital, Mrs. Garza?"

"Your sister, Anna," Mrs. Garza's tears began to flow. "It was a drunk driver. He hit the passenger side. Your sister Dolores was killed instantly. She felt little pain," Mrs. Garza said with her face looking down, her hands over her face. "I'm so sorry. There was nothing they could do for her."

"Oh, my God! Dolores! Dolores! Please, no, no puede

ser." sobbed Anna.

Laura and Thelma quickly wrapped their arms around her.

"Dolores, what will I do without you? Dolores, please, come back. Don't leave me. It can't be. Please." Anna fell uncontrollably to her knees. "Take me to them, now!"

Anna's cry could be heard all through the house. Laura's neighbors came out to observe the commotion. To Anna, Dolores was her life, her direction; they were part of each other. She felt as if her soul had been ripped out.

The funeral ceremonies for Dolores began the following day. Thelma and Laura never left Anna's side. Anna's mom was weak from the accident. Her younger brother Joey had both legs broken, and he sat in the first pew the entire procession.

The funeral parlor had standing room only. Dolores had many friends. The entire school had been dismissed. The students clung together trying to come to grips with the tragedy. Dolores had received so many beautiful wreaths that the funeral director had to put many of them in the van to take to the cemetery. Thelma's mom had to be sedated to calm her down. That was the only way the doctors would agree to let her attend the funeral service. Laura and her family stood a few pews behind Anna's family. Anna was in anguish. In seconds Anna's entire family had become incomplete and would forever mourn the loss of their sweet daughter and sister.

Anna was oblivious to the people hugging her and their sentiments of sorrow. She stared at the casket, afraid to remove her eyes from it. If she did, Dolores would surely disappear forever.

Laura turned back and caught a glimpse of Thelma with her parents.

It was Anna's turn to pay her last respects to Dolores. Anna and her parents kneeled next to the casket. The pink, shiny casket looked plush. It seemed for a second that Dolores smiled at Anna. Anna's heart jumped as if Dolores would wake up. Anna's father put his hand over Anna's shoulder while her mother hugged her tightly. Anna did not remove her eyes from her sister's body. Even in death, her rosy cheeks came to life. The bruises sustained from the accident were skillfully hidden with make-up. Dolores' long lashes, full lips, and high cheekbones only added to her beauty. Anna grabbed her dead sister's hand one last time and slipped a family picture in it. In the picture she had her arms wrapped around Dolores.

"Don't forget about me, Dolores." Tears began to run down Anna's tired face. At the same moment, the entire room of people began to cry. It was as if for that moment everyone could feel Anna's deep pain at the loss of her sister.

Anna kneeled and rested her head on the casket. Once again, a calm, comfortable gust rushed through her body. She felt a strong embrace once more. Anna looked at Dolores' face and realized instantly that what she felt that Saturday afternoon in Laura's backyard had been her sister saying good-bye. It happened the exact moment Dolores passed away. The feeling was an unexplainable, joyous one, a feeling Anna would ponder all of her life. It left her feeling both peaceful and empty.

Anna's mother hugged her. Her daddy once again put

his hand on Anna's shoulder. Her brother Joey remained in the first pew. Mrs. Guzmán whispered, "Good-bye my dear, sweet daughter. Que te perdone Diosito. Go with the angels my little girl."

At the church, the priest led the mass and tried desperately to make sense of this senseless and tragic death.

"It's the devil who causes accidents, not God. It is the devil that tries to take souls, hoping they are not ready to go." In Spanish he said, "Es el diablo que causa accidentes, no es Diosito."

Anna held her brother's hand during mass. She looked into his empty eyes and quickly was reminded of the horrible shock Joey must have had, witnessing his sister's death. Anna knew that Dolores was safe and happy wherever her soul was. Someday, she'd meet with her again. For now, it was too painful to think about the rest of her life without her sister. As the priest finished the mass, he said, "God has a place for Dolores. May she rest in peace."

Anna closed her eyes and envisioned Dolores in her white, beaded, long-sleeved, tea-length dress. She looked beautiful in it when she wore it to the sweetheart dance. She looked exquisite now as she lay in her plush casket, forever young and beautiful.

During the following two weeks, the evenings consisted of rosarios. Thelma's and Laura's parents kindly dropped the girls off, so they could be with Anna. Catholics, especially in the Latin community, believe that although the soul has passed on to heaven, it wouldn't hurt to pray for the deceased soul, just in case it didn't quite make it. These rosarios should ensure Dolores of salvation. Thelma, Laura, and Anna stood by each other until the last day of the rosarios. Friendship in the Latino community goes deep within the soul. As a result of this tragic death, their lives would be bonded forever.

Anna continued to mourn the loss of her oldest and dearest sister Dolores. It is ironic that from the empty part in her heart, Anna seemed to grow strength. Every time Anna competed in her U.I.L. competition, there seemed to be the spirit of two. It didn't matter where or in what she competed—all district prose and poetry or acting in plays—she would always bring back a ribbon or trophy. Anna went to the state finals and one time made it to the nationals in the acting and prose division. Each time she came back, she'd place the trophies by Dolores' trophy case. Every time Anna won, she felt happy and content. It was therapy for her. The room they once shared looked like a shrine for Dolores; only instead of filling the room with candles and crosses, Anna filled it with trophies. You could hardly walk into her room.

Anna's parents talked to a counselor about her behavior. He told them Anna was still mourning the death of her sister. As long as she didn't think she was Dolores, there was no harm. In fact, it was good therapy. This also helped Joey and his parents mourn for Dolores. There was a sort of comfort in knowing she had not been forgotten by any of the family members. They were told to be patient and wait for Anna to pass this stage.

Anna had placed a photograph of Dolores and one of herself next to each other. Whenever Mrs. Guzmán entered the room, she could not help but notice the striking resemblance between her daughters. Only time would heal the pain.

The years flew by quickly. Laura, Thelma, and Anna had now become sophomores at San Manuel High. Anna awoke from a good night's sleep. As she lay in her bed, she pondered the many triumphs her trophies represented. She stared at Dolores' trophies, then at Dolores' picture. She thought, "I will always love you, Dolores; but look at my room. It's too crowded. I know you'll understand."

The telephone rang. Laura picked up the telephone. "Hello."

"Hello, Laura."

"Hi, Anna. What's up?" There was a slight hesitation, "Anna, are you there?"

"I've decided it's time to take the trophies out of my room. I realized this morning. I can hardly walk in this room. I'm ready, Laura. I feel it. I am ready to move on."

Laura could hardly believe the words coming from the receiver.

"Laura, Laura, are you there?" Anna asked.

"Anna, I'll be right over." Laura was thrilled Anna had finally accepted her sister's death after so many years. Mr. and Mrs. Guzmán did not question her judgement. They were relieved and ready to begin to live life again. Dolores' picture remained on the wall to keep her memory alive. But the removal of the trophies was welcomed. A look of peace and joy swept through Joey's eyes as he carefully helped put the trophies in boxes. Together, Mr. and Mrs. Guzmán, Joey, Laura, and Anna moved the trophies from Dolores' room to the attic. It was as if Anna had finally healed from her sister's death. In her own way, she had happily fulfilled her promise to herself and to her sister. She was ready to move on with her life.

That sacred summer was one to be remembered by the Guzmán family. The summers now seemed longer as the inseparable threesome shrank to two. Thelma and her family migrated north every May. The girls wrote letters to each other. They wrote about boys they had crushes on. For Thelma, writing two letters, one to Laura and one to Anna, quickly became tiresome. She had to wake up early in the morning and came home late in the evening. It was agreed that Thelma would address one letter to both Anna and Laura, and the problem was resolved.

Thelma's letters were short and spoke mostly about the work she did up north. She was up as early as 5:00 a.m and would often get home as late as 9:00 p.m. Anna wrote to Thelma asking her to tell Laura and her exactly what it was she and her family did up north. Why was it so important they go every summer? Why couldn't they take a summer off or maybe even go on vacation? If they went to make money, couldn't they save it and come home early and take a vacation? Anna's questions were naive. Thelma wrote a letter back explaining as best she could what they did in North Dakota and why.

Dearest Silly, Naive Anna,

How are you and Laura? I don't suppose Laura put you up to this, although I suspect she is as curious as you are as to what we do up north. I'll explain it as best I can.

When we get here from Texas, we are provided with a three-bedroom home. That is part of the farmer's arrangement with the farm workers. We have to share the house with another family, one bathroom, one bath, one stove. As you can imagine, it is not much fun. I'll spare you the gross details of filth and move on to the farming.

I've written to you that we don't always get the same family, and we don't always get along. This year's family is okay. They're from the valley. My mom has to wake up at 4:30 a.m. to beat the other lady to the stove. Sometimes she gets beaten to the stove, and the result is cold sandwiches for lunch. I really dislike that. I'll spare the waiting in line to go to the bathroom and washing up a bit.

My mom sends my younger brother and sister to school.

I truly wish I could be there with you two.

The plants we are thinning are sugar beets. The worst part is making sure the sugar beets are at least ten inches apart. Our job is to make sure to check that the plant is small, about eight inches tall, and that they're not too close to each other. If they are, we must thin them with a hoe. Otherwise they may drain the nutrients, and not one will be good enough to sell.

The farmers pay us by the acre. We finish around forty-five acres every five weeks among my parents and four older siblings. When you're through thinning the plants, after about a month, you go back and weed the plant. After the plant grows to full term, you pull out stickers, etc.

Many times, I hope for cloud cover because of the hot

sun. Mornings are cold.

The only day we have off is Sunday. Thank God for Sundays. That is the day I get to rest and catch up on my reading. I go into town, and I usually buy a book each month.

I hope I have given you a better understanding of what it's like to be a farm worker. It gets lonely up here. There really isn't anyone to talk to except Myra, my silly sister. She is boring. Anyway, I have to go now.

Write back soon.

P.S. I have callouses on my hand, and my back hurts at times. Mom tells me I don't drink enough water.

Your friend,

Thelma

The drive home from North Dakota to Texas took three days. For Thelma, it was an eternity. She couldn't wait to come home. As the years passed, new friends came between the threesome; but, in the end, the circle and many years of solid, true friendship would never be broken. When Thelma returned from North Dakota, they had their usual celebration at Pizza Hut, catching up on the latest gossip their small town had to offer. Who's dating whom? What's going on where? This always seemed delightful to Thelma.

CHAPTER TWO

Five Years Later. . .

As the high school pep rally began, the varsity cheerleaders ran to the middle of the gym. They excited the students and cheered the players on to victory. Anna, as usual, shined. The crowd roared with amazement, as Anna took center stage and performed her gymnastic feats, performing consecutive, graceful flip flops from one side of the gym to the other. The crowd was enthralled with the 5-feet-3-inch, energetic beauty. Anna loved them back.

Thelma and Laura stood on the bleachers designated for juniors, cheering the team on with the rest of their friends. It was early February; and, although pep rallies had been designated only for the football team, Mr. Zuniga, the principal, suggested a pep rally for the varsity basketball players. They had been district champs for two years in a row. Laura's eyes flashed flirtatiously toward Danny, who sat with the basketball varsity team. Her heart jumped excitedly as he flashed a smile toward her.

Next week would be their three-year anniversary of dating each other. Laura was completely taken by Danny López; he stood 6 feet 2 inches tall with a slender body and white, milky skin. His emerald green eyes mesmerized her; their smiling appearance always made her feel comfortable. Because she was 5 feet 7 inches, she loved the fact that she could look up at him and loved it when he towered over her.

His strong, large hands and arms overwhelmed her. She was overtaken by his touch. Her almond-shaped, brown eyes and long dark lashes could not help but blink coyishly when he looked directly at her and ran his fingers through her dark brown, healthy hair. Her parents adored him, and his accepted her. How athletic he looked in his gold and white uniform as he sat in the middle of the gym. Though there were other players and commotion going on, Laura stood dumbfounded by him.

Thelma nudged Laura softly, "Laura, hello."

Laura quickly came back to reality. She smiled, sheepishly. Her bright white, straight teeth; her smile; and her look displayed Laura's thoughts.

"Yes, what?" Laura asked.

"Nothing, just your gaga eyes toward Danny were getting too silly," Thelma answered.

Thelma's round, hazel eyes and round face gave a look of sarcasm. Laura didn't mind.

As the crowd roared and the bleachers moved, she remembered the nauseating feelings she'd been experiencing the last couple of days; and the dizzy spell she had as she and Thelma climbed the bleachers. If these had happened monthly, she would have dismissed the pain and feelings as stomach flu. But these feelings were persistent for the last three weeks.

She drove to a distant town, careful and discrete so that no one saw her purchase a self-pregnancy test. She felt bad, but she needed to make sure she was not pregnant. Laura was almost 99 percent sure that it was stomach flu and that the congestion in her nose caused her to loose her balance going up the bleachers. She was positive that was the explanation. But just in case, she'd make sure. She was seventeen now. It would be silly to be pregnant at that age.

As Laura walked into her bedroom and kicked her shoes into the closet, she glanced at the clock. 8:30 p.m. "I'd better take that darned pregnancy test," she said to herself. Laura followed the directions as best she could. She put the tube under the bathroom sink and went to make a sandwich for herself.

"Hi, mom."

"Hi, sugar. Why so late?"

"Oh, basketball. I'm in journalism. I have to take pictures."

"Yes," Mrs. Garza said as her eyes grew with sarcasm. "Did you take any pictures of the rest of the team or just Danny?"

"Mom," said Laura with a smile.

Mrs. Garza smiled. "Just joking."

"Anything in the mail for me, Mom? I'm waiting for the results of the college entrance exams." Laura fumbled through the refrigerator. "Yes, they should be here. I heard Fred and Hilda saying they received their test scores already."

Mrs. Garza finished her glass of milk and put it on the sink. "Don't worry. Yours are in the mail."

Laura finished making her sandwich and threw some chips on the plate. "I'm going to my room, Mom. I need to finish up on some work, okay."

Laura quickly locked the door behind her and walked to the bathroom. She saw that the urine sample had turned blue. She rubbed her eyes and shook the tube desperately, hoping it would somehow change color.

"Oh, my God, please."

In an instant Laura began to tremble. "This can't be," she thought. She read the instructions again. They said, "For best results use a morning urine sample."

"Yes, yes, this isn't accurate. It can't be accurate. I'll sleep and—and—and take it again tomorrow morning," she said frantically as she turned the light switch off and went to sleep.

CHAPTER THREE

The morning light slipped in through Laura's bedroom window as she rolled over and turned the alarm clock off. "Seven o'clock so soon," she thought to herself. "Let me sleep one more hour, please," she said irritated. She put the pillow over her face to keep the morning sunlight out of her eyes. She had been unable to sleep a wink. She'd tossed and turned the whole night with worry. Laura's period was late, but that happened once in a while when Laura was under stress due to school competition or tests. She thought it was nothing to worry about. "Besides, what's a few weeks late mean anyway? It surely could not happen to me," she assured herself.

Suddenly, Laura jumped out of her bed as if a stranger had entered her room. Her face was filled with fear. She ran to her bathroom sink. "Oh, my God, this isn't happening. Please, I'll be good for the rest of my life," she said quietly as tears fell. Her nightmare was coming true. She felt her heart beating. She stood and looked unwittingly toward last week's pregnancy test. The test showed a faded blue color. According to the test directions, that meant she was pregnant. "Okay," thought Laura desperately, "The results could be wrong. I took the test last night; the test says for best results, do it in the morning. I'll just do it right now," she said to herself. She reached nervously for the container. Almost simultaneously, she began to cough; and a sudden urge to vomit made her go down on her knees. She quickly hugged the toilet and regurgitated. Laura felt numb as tears ran down her face. There seemed to be no reason to retest. To Laura, reality had struck like a hurricane from all directions.

Laura put her hands to her face. "Please, I don't want to be pregnant. What will I do with a baby?" She looked at herself in the mirror. "Oh, my gosh! I look like a zombie!" she cried as she wiped her hands over her face in disbelief.

"Why me? Why me? I know I'm not the only teenager who does more than kiss with her stupid boyfriend. I took care of myself. Danny wore protection most of the time. How could this have happened? This just cannot happen right now; I have plans for the future." She frantically began to put make-up on her face to get ready for school. "Why did I have to be the unlucky one?" she thought as she crossed her arms. She finished dressing and prepared to walk out of her bedroom. Suddenly, she shivered frantically.

"My God. OH! NO! What have I done? What about my parents. They worked so hard to get me where I am today," she anguished in silence.

Laura's face was flush with panic. "What about my friends and relatives and what about the neighbors, those gossiping neighbors. They'll have something to talk about for the rest of the year," she thought quietly.

Laura Garza, sweet little Laura Garza. Such high hopes. "She's going to be a doctor someday," bragged her mom proudly to her neighbor, Mrs. Riley. How proud would she be now of her ignorant daughter Laura? The neighbors would surely laugh and talk about her. Mom would surely be hurt and terribly embarrassed.

"I have to talk to someone," she thought desperately.

"I can't...I can't!" she said loudly, as if two people were in her head, "I can never tell anybody. If the students find out at school, I'll be considered a freak, a loser, a joke by everyone at school. I have let my parents down."

"I can't. I simply cannot tell anyone. I won't ruin my life for a baby. It wasn't my fault; it was Danny's. That's all there is to it."

Laura's dad knocked softly on her bedroom door. "Are you okay, Laura?" Laura nearly jumped.

"Honey, is there someone with you?"

Laura gasped nervously, "Why would you ask a silly question like that, Dad?"

"I heard you talking."

"I...I...I was talking to Anna on the telephone," she replied as she opened her bedroom door.

CHAPTER FOUR

Well, hurry up and come to breakfast. It's getting late, and I don't want to be late for work," said her daddy in a pleasant manner.

"Good morning, Dad," she said as she walked to the kitchen and as she reached over and hugged him around the neck.

"Good morning, chula. Aren't you going to eat breakfast?"

"No thanks, Dad. I don't feel so great this morning."

"Where's Mom?" she asked as she reached across the breakfast table and poured juice in the glass.

"She left early and took Sandra and Peter with her to school. She left a note for you. I think it's from Danny."

Just then, Laura felt an irritable, nauseating pain rise up from her stomach. She accidently dropped her glass.

"Are you all right," asked her dad worriedly.

"I'm fine. I'm fine. That's what I get for being in a rush," she said as she quickly grabbed the paper towels and began to wipe the juice from the floor.

"Never mind that," said her dad as he stared at her face. "Your face is as white as chalk. It's as if you had the biggest scare of your life."

She looked up annoyed. "No, Dad," retorted Laura, raising her voice in agitation. "It's just my paranoia getting the best of me."

"What?" he asked with a frown of confusion on his face. "Paranoid, about what?" Suddenly his thin lips curved into a smile.

"Oh, I know," he burst out laughing as if he knew the answer to her anxiety. "Your exams. Am I right?"

"What are you talking about?" she asked as she stood up from the floor.

"Yeah! This week is the week. You'll find out how well you did on your college entrance exams for next year."

Laura suddenly felt the horrible knot once again surface from her stomach, accompanied with the need to vomit. As she ran past the kitchen and into the hall bathroom, she shut the door and began vomiting. Tears of shame stung her eyes. Feelings of total defeat, failure, and nervousness ran through her mind.

"Laura," said her dad softly through the bathroom door. "Why are you so nervous?" She quickly rinsed out her mouth and tried to compose herself. As she opened the bathroom door and timidly ran her fingers through her hair, she said, "You're right. This test...this college entrance exam has me really nervous."

Her dad gave a half grin and said, "Remember this, my little girl. It's your junior year. If you don't do well, you still have another year to sharpen your test skills."

Laura could not make eye contact with her dad. She looked down. "Yeah, you're right Dad," she said, desperately holding back her tears. If you don't mind, I don't feel very good today. Would it be all right if I stayed home from school today?" She placed her hands over her stomach.

"Sure, I'll call your mom and let her know."

"OH! NO! Please don't. I don't want to bother her. It's probably just a stomach virus going around."

He put his hand over his mouth and rubbed it, thinking the situation over. "Well, okay. But if it gets worse, you call your mom. All right, Laura? I'll see you later." He walked out the front door.

Laura walked to her bedroom and lay on her bed. "Entrance exam, hah," she thought. That was the farthest thing from her mind. In fact, it wasn't even on her mind, not since yesterday.

Still devastated from the shock, she sat in bed and pictured how her future would be if she had the baby. " No," she thought as she rolled over to one side. "I'd prefer to drop out of school or even run away before I'd submit to such humiliation from the world. Damn you! Damn you, Danny!" she said angrily as tears began to fall down her face once again. "I hate you for this."

Her nausea continued and forced her into a fetal position. Bringing her arms around her knees, she moaned, "Why do I feel so bad?"

The next morning was a replay of the one before. "I can't go on like this. This is a nightmare," she thought as she pressed her hands to her face.

The chore of waking up every morning and dragging herself to the bathroom was agonizing. But soon, Laura had mastered her secret. She no longer stayed home. That was the only way she was able to convince her mom not to send her to the doctor. Her morning sickness was not as dreadful now that she had accepted her fate. As she stood looking at her flushed face in the mirror, she noticed the circles under her eyes had enlarged and darkened.

Laura walked across the bedroom and read the calendar. She murmured quietly to herself, "February the 3rd is when I received my pregnancy results. We are now March the 3rd. That would make me four weeks pregnant."

She looked down at her stomach. Although there were no visible signs, she felt that she was gaining weight. She stretched the T-shirt away from her body to give her a feeling of comfort. The fact that she was 5 feet 7 inches and weighed 115 pounds helped her feel at ease with her secret.

Laura returned for a last glance of herself in the mirror. She stroked make-up on her face to cover the dark circles around her eyes and the light brown spots which appeared around her cheeks. She was amazed at how no one had discovered her pregnancy. The excuse, accepted by her mom, peers, and boyfriend, was a severe bout of the flu.

A light knock came from her door. "Laura, may I come in?" asked her mother. "How are you feeling?"

"Much better, Mom, really."

"Well, you really did have most of us worried. Laura,

may I ask you something?" asked her mom curiously.

"Sure, Mom, shoot," she replied, as she brushed her long, thick, wavy brown hair.

"Have you and Danny broken up?"

As she put mascara over her long, curly lashes to distract from her fatigued, weary eyes, Laura turned with a half smile and replied, "Why would you ask that?"

"Well, the fact that he's been calling and you haven't returned his calls is a big hint," she remarked sarcastically.

"Mom, I've just been really busy." Laura stroked the blush over her round face.

"Are you seeing another guy, Laura Garza?"

A smile suddenly appeared on Laura's face causing the lipstick to extend beyond the lip line.

"Oh, Mom! Now look what you made me do. Besides, I think I'm entitled to some privacy."

"All right. Okay. I won't snoop for answers anymore. Don't forget your breakfast. You know it's brain power," she said to Laura as she walked out of the room.

"I know, Mom. How could I forget? You've told us for years."

Laura walked to the kitchen and poured herself a glass of milk. She peeked outside the window and waved good-bye to her parents, Sandra, and Peter, as they drove off to work and school.

She looked at her wrist watch. "Anna should be here any

minute."

Suddenly the phone rang. Laura quickly picked it up. "Hello. Laura, is that you?" asked a deep, male voice on the other end. "Laura, please don't hang up. Talk to me. I know you're there. Why are you angry at me? What have I done?" he asked in a confused tone.

"Nothing! Nothing is wrong!" she replied angrily. She gripped the receiver so tightly she could feel her neck muscles becoming tense.

"Listen, I have to get to school. I have to hang up. I'll see you around."

"Hey, wait. Don't hang up. The last time we spoke, you said you loved me. You don't sound as if you feel that way anymore. Where did you go last night?"

Drained from the torture of her secret, she retorted angrily, "Danny, I don't want to talk to you right now. I've got to go."

Laura slammed the telephone and walked out of the house just as Anna was driving up the driveway.

"Hi, Laura," said Anna.

"Good morning, Anna," Laura answered. She threw Anna's cheerleading pom-poms to the back seat as she stepped into the car. "What a mess you have here!"

"Are you going to the party tonight?" asked Anna, totally oblivious to Laura's whining.

"What party?" asked Laura.

"Diana's party, remember? And are you going to go with me, or did you and Danny make up?"

Laura answered disgustedly, "I'm not up to it, so you can skip me on this one."

"But it's Friday, time to rock and roll," said Anna as she drove with one hand on the steering wheel and tapped the other on her knee to a beat only she understood. "We'll we're here." They drove into the parking lot of San Manuel High.

"I don't know. I'll think about it," said Laura trying to evade the situation.

As they walked into the entrance doors of their school, Anna gave Laura a nudge.

"Wait just a minute. I need to fix my hair." Anna quickly grabbed her long, sandy-brown hair and expertly wound a rubber band around it. This exposed her round face. Her emerald-green blouse highlighted her green, almond-shaped eyes. What she didn't have in height, she made up with beauty and personality.

"Hurry up! Come on. We're going to be late for class," said Laura as she hurried Anna toward the lockers.

"Hey, listen," said Anna hastily, "Yesterday at cheerleading practice, I fixed it to where Rosie Galván and I will be at the top of the pyramid for the pictures. This way, when you come from your photography class, we'll all be ready for the annual picture."

Laura giggled, "What are you talking about, you nut? Once again, it's called journalism, not photography class."

"Well, you know what I'm talking about," remarked

Anna absentmindedly.

"Listen, get to class now. I'll see you during lunch," said Laura.

"What do you mean?" remarked Anna sarcastically. "You're not having lunch with Dan the man?"

"I haven't for a long time now; you know that. Bye-bye now."

Laura sat in her fourth-period class counting the minutes to the bell. "Time to go have lunch," she told Rosie Galván as she quickly maneuvered her way down the hall.

"Hey, Laura. Wait up. What's your rush?"

"I feel really hungry today."

"You felt really hungry yesterday and the day before that."

Rosie gently grabbed Laura's shoulder, "Should we wait for the girls and decide where we'll be having lunch?"

"What's to decide? The cafeteria is fine with me."

"What. No pizza for Laura?" remarked Rosie teasingly.

"No. Don't get me wrong. I love pizza. It's the time. I don't want to wait that long. I feel I'm about to faint if I don't have something soon." Laura did not know that the reason she felt hungrier than usual was because of her pregnancy.

"Hey, look. I see Anna and Thelma." Rosie waved her hand as high as she could.

"Did they see you?" asked Laura.

"Catch up to us in the lunch line!" yelled Laura.

"Laura, don't forget. Today you have to take pictures of the cheerleading squad."

"Don't worry, I won't forget," said Laura. She put her tray on the table.

"Hello, Thelma," said Rosie as she opened her milk carton.

"What have you been up to? It's been a while since I've seen you. Where have you been?" Thelma's weary face displayed no emotion as she sat her tired body on the chair. She looked like an athlete that had been overworked and needed a rest.

"My dad hurt his back last week at work. Since he is the bread winner in our family, no money is coming in. Since I am the oldest, my dad thought it would be a good idea for me to help out. A family friend happens to own El Rey restaurant, and he was nice enough to give me a job. So that's where I've been the last week and for the rest of the month." She paused for a while. "We'll migrate a little later this year due to Dad's accident. That's good. I hate migrating. It puts a damper in my life. I wish my family wouldn't have to move every year. Since I am the oldest, Dad expects a lot more from me." She tossed her thin, black hair over her shoulder and remarked with a proud smirk on her tired face. "That's okay. I can handle it."

Rosie, Anna, and Laura listened with empathy.

"Thelma, will you have time for debate after school?" Laura swallowed her last bite of enchilada. "Don't forget, we want to repeat our state championship status for U.I.L. next year."

Thelma looked down at her plate and ignored the question.

"Thelma, you didn't answer my question," repeated Laura.

Thelma looked toward Laura. Her hazel eyes looked up with disappointment, "I don't think I'll be able to join the debate team next year, so there's no reason to practice anymore. I'm not even sure I'll finish my senior year next year." Thelma's voice became shaky, her eyes teary.

Anna, Rosie, and Laura sat stunned and horrified. Anna put her fork down on her tray.

"You what! You may not be coming back to school again? That's crazy! You and Laura have been in the National Honor Society for the last three years. Next year both of you will receive scholarships galore. What are you saying? Your dream, since we were in fourth grade, was always—and to this day—to some day become a lawyer. You're going to throw it all away. Listen to what you're saying, girl!" exclaimed Anna.

Despite the raucous cafeteria, the girls remained totally immersed in their conversation, as if no one existed.

"I know what I'm saying, Anna, and sometimes dreams have to be put aside when reality sets in," said Thelma maturely, though her voice cracked.

The girls emptied their trays. As the girls sat on the bench sipping their drinks, Anna sharply grabbed Laura and whispered, "Look, there goes Danny with Julio and Eddie. He's looking this way. Now he's going the other direction." Anna looked at Laura directly in the eye.

"Let's go drink a Coke at the snack bar," said Laura as

she put her arm around Thelma's shoulder.

"Laura, you and I have been friends forever. If something is bothering you, I have the right to know. We've shared each other's deepest secrets and know more about each other than our own mothers," she said throwing her hands up in the air. "I think it's time you told me what's going on with you and Danny. Is there someone else?"

Laura ran her fingers through her hair and tossed her hair over her shoulders.

"Listen, you're blowing this out of proportion. Danny and I haven't broken up. There is a problem, but I don't want to tell you right now. We'll talk about it later. I don't want to be late for class."

"When later?" asked Anna as the fifth-period bell rang, and they walked to their designated classes.

"Whew!" thought Laura to herself as she managed once again to elude Anna's questioning.

CHAPTER FIVE

*L*aura gave a sigh of relief. "Good afternoon, Laura. It's very nice to see you walking in before the bell rings and not after," remarked Mrs. De León jokingly.

"I tried my very best today," Laura replied as she walked to her desk and put her books and purse down.

"Susie, are you going to be my assigned partner for today?" she asked while preparing the camera and film in the darkroom.

"Yes, I am. We're assigned the cheerleading squad today."

"Everyone have a seat," continued Mrs. De León. "Absenteeism has really been down these past six weeks," smiled Mrs. De León, as she leaned down and marked her grade book. "Well, class, you all have your assignments. Is everyone ready? Check your equipment. If you are not sure about your assignment, it's up on the board."

"Laura and Susie," directed Mrs. De León.

"Yes, Mrs. De León," replied the girls.

"Since you will be going out to the gym today, I have assigned you the basketball team as well." Laura's jaw dropped as she realized she would have to confront Danny. Mrs. De León continued, "I want to make sure each one of you is aware of what you are doing. I don't want to hear any reports about horsing around. You go into the class, take the pictures, and come right back," she said bluntly, pacing around the room making sure the students handled their equipment properly.

Laura yawned and hoped that Danny would not be in the gym even though that was the exact time the athletics class met.

For a moment she hesitated and wanted desperately to ask Mrs. De León if she would change her assignment.

"Well, are you ready?"

Laura turned, responding to the right tap on her shoulder from Susie Atkins. Susie's warm, blue eyes indicated readiness. Her blond hair, accented by her tall, slim body, made it seem as if she should be the one being photographed. Last year Laura and Susie were approached by a local modeling agency, but neither was interested in the offer.

The girls walked toward the gym. "Hey, Laura. I was thinking. If you like, you can take the pictures of the basketball players; and I can do the cheerleaders. This way you and Danny can talk and be with each other."

"What are you talking about?" Laura asked nervously, "Why would you say that?"

Susie pushed her hair away from her face and said embarrassingly, "I passed by the hall this afternoon, and I couldn't help but notice that you and Danny aren't together anymore. You know how gossip spreads fast in this small school, Laura."

"And what else did you notice?" continued Laura flabbergasted.

"Well, I'm not the only one who has noticed it. The whole school has noticed."

"Aha, and what is everybody saying?"

Susie looked down, not wanting to tell Laura what the rumors were.

Laura shifted her camera from one arm to the other and said, "Susie, I know you better than that. What has Danny been saying about me?"

"No, it's not Danny."

"Well, who is it? Come on. This is such a small town. When your parents are in an argument, the whole town seems to know."

Laura, her face twisting in anger, stopped Susie right before they opened the doors to the gym. She grabbed Susie by the shoulder and once again demanded an answer, as if Laura's life depended on it.

"Who are they? Who's starting the rumors?"

Susie ran her fingers through her hair and reluctantly said, "Okay, if you want to know, it's Daisy and María."

"What?" Laura said as her eyes grew large. Her face was full of dismay. "Those girls ought to spend time trying to save their own reputations."

"Daisy was telling the whole class how you and Danny yelled at each other in the hall and that you slapped him."

"I did what?" Laura turned away in disgust.

"Wait, Laura, there's more. The reason you've broken up

is because he's been dating someone else. And he broke up with you in the hall in front of everyone. You were so embarrassed you took off running like a mad woman."

Laura paced back and forth as she murmured, "I can't believe it." Laura was in a daze as she walked into the gym. The cheerleaders weren't ready. That gave her a while to compose herself and to absorb the terrible, tacky gossip circulating around school.

"Laura, can you hear me? I've been talking to you," Susie remarked as she focused her camera on some of the basketball players who were coming out of the boys' dressing room.

"Don't pay attention to gossip. We all know how those girls are. Most people listen and take it with a grain of salt. Rumors are just that. Hey, I'm sure you've heard some of the rumors about Jacob Mason and me. We just don't let it bother us. If you ignore it, before you know it, they're gossiping about someone else. Don't worry. Everything is going to turn out just great between you and Danny."

"If only things were great between Danny and me," she thought. If only it weren't true. The gossip she heard was a lot better than if the real truth were to be discovered.

"Hey, Laura, cheer up. I'm going to take a picture of Jacob and Danny together, since they are first string and since Danny is the captain. Not bad for a junior, huh?"

A deep feeling of alarm ran down to the pit of Laura's stomach. She had failed to think about Danny's career and what a tragic effect this could have on his future.

"Laura, are you all right? You're shaking. Your face is as white as chalk."

"It's nothing. I just have to go to the bathroom to get a drink of water. I'll be right back."

"Let me walk you."

"No, don't be silly," said Laura as tears suddenly began to run down her face. She didn't understand these feelings. Why was she crying so easily, and why were her breasts tender? If she asked anyone, then everyone would find out. She wasn't so sure she wanted the problems associated with having a baby.

"Hey, Cristina! Have you seen my pom-poms?" yelled Anna from across the lockers in the girls' gym.

Laura hurriedly threw water on her face before any more misfortunes occurred.

"Girls, the photographers are here!" yelled Cristina, as she looked into the mirror and added the finishing touches to her make-up. She carefully outlined her lips with her fingers to make sure that the lipstick was in its proper place. She brushed her straight, brown hair and gave it that perfect, shiny, finishing touch. "That will do it," Cristina smiled quite confidently.

Laura found the best place in the gym to take pictures just as the cheerleading squad walked into the gym.

A cheerful voice from among the squad yelled, "Laura, my dear. I am so glad you were able to be here."

A warm glow and a comforting smile came from Laura's face as she recognized the mischievous voice behind it. "Hi, old friend," remarked Anna as she hugged Laura and whispered in her ear. "Don't forget to ask to take a picture with Rosie and me on top of the pyramid."

"Hello, Laura."

"Hi, Michelle."

"Hi, Laura."

"Hi, Daisy and María," she said with a slight strain in her voice. She remembered the awful gossip circulating around the school was due to them. Confronting them would only make things worse. She just had to endure.

"Okay, girls. Since you all were U.C.A. South Texas champs, I'd like to take a picture of the winning pyramid and then individual shots."

"Which pyramid should we do?" asked Michelle, a confident, bright, and pretty girl.

She stood only 5 feet 2 inches tall with black hair and dark brown eyes. She was nothing spectacular to look at; but because she was so nice and had a beautiful disposition, she was liked by everyone. Voted most popular the last three years, Michelle had been elected head cheerleader by the team these same three years. She seemed to have it all together. She was never part of the gossip circles.

"Why don't we do the pyramid we've been practicing?" asked Anna, kicking away her pom-poms.

"Yes, that's fine. All our faces will show," replied Michelle.

"I thought it would be a good idea to take the picture in the middle of the gym where the San Manuel tiger mascot will be seen. It will match your gold and white uniforms and add more color to the picture," said Laura.

"Laura," interrupted Susie, "where are you going to take a picture of the basketball team?"

"Susie, I'm really busy with the cheerleaders. Why don't you find a nice spot, and you take a picture of them? You know you can do it. After the group shot, take a picture of them individually."

"Where do you want for us to take the pictures?" asked Daisy.

"As I was saying, I'd like you girls by the south wall where the tiger mascot picture will show. It will match your gold and white uniforms and add more color to the picture."

"That sounds great," replied María.

Anna flashed Laura a thumbs up for suggesting the 3-2-1 pyramid, which put her on top.

Susie walked up alongside Laura as they finished their jobs and headed back to class.

"Oh, listen. I almost forgot. Danny said he'd like to talk to you. He said to please wait for him by the locker room after school. Let's go leave the cameras in class. Oh, another thing," she continued with her arms up in the air. "Where is my mind today?" she remarked as she pulled out a carefully folded paper from her pocket. "He asked me to give you this. It must be a love note," she said teasingly.

"Thanks."

"No problem."

"Well, aren't you going to read it?"

"No, not now," Laura said nervously as she put the note in her purse.

"Hey, Laura, wait up!" yelled Anna. "What are you up to?"

"Nothing much. We're just heading back to class."

"Well, aren't you going to tell your buddy?"

Laura's face grew confused. "Tell her what?"

"You know. The note that Danny wrote to you?"

Anna's eyes grew with interest.

"You guys. It's just a note. What a tattletale!" Laura remarked jokingly as she swung her purse toward Susie.

"My goodness, Susie. We ought to nickname you the school newspaper. Will you stop already?"

Laura swung her purse at her a second time. Laughingly, Susie replied, "All right, okay. See you tomorrow."

"Go on, you silly nut," said Anna.

"Hmmm. So I guess you and Danny will kiss and make up, huh?"

"You guessed wrong. I'm not sure what I'll do until I figure out what to do."

Anna exchanged her pom-poms from one hand to another. A look of confusion came over Anna's freckled face. "Well, are you going to read the letter?"

Laura looked down at her camera and once again avoided Anna's question. "I have to go leave the camera in class. Then I have speech practice after school."

Anna looked at her watch. "It's four o'clock. I have cheerleading practice tryouts for next year. I'll come by the speech department and pick you up at about five. Does that sound fine?"

"We'll go to the Stars and have a bite to eat. Sounds good, Anna. See ya."

When Laura reached her locker, her fingers spryly opened the combination lock. Suddenly, she felt a soft, gentle touch to her waist, followed by a deep, sweet voice saying, "I'm glad you could meet me here."

Laura froze. She could not move. She longed for his touch and wanted badly to turn around and hug him. She also knew if she did, she'd have to tell him what was going on; and she couldn't do that. Instead, tears of despair ran down her face.

"Laura, for God's sake, please tell me what's going on with you. I don't know what I've done that deserves such cold punishment," said Danny as he turned her around to face him.

"Baby, why are you crying?" He cupped her face with his hands and gently kissed her on the forehead.

"Look at me." His gentle, brown eyes were filled with questions.

As Laura raised her eyes and looked up at Danny's tall frame, handsome face, and full lips, her fear subsided. Their tall, slim bodies seemed as one as they began to embrace. Laura thought she could stand it no longer. She swung her arms around his shoulders like a child who was terrified. "Oh Danny, I'm so scared."

Danny frowned, "Scared of what, Laura?"

Laura's face looked worried. "Nothing, it's nothing. Just hold me."

"Everything will be all right as soon as you tell me the problem."

"Hold me just a little longer."

Laura and Danny stayed intertwined in each other's arms; a kiss was inevitable. As his lips met hers, burning passion seemed to come alive. Laura welcomed his kiss desperately. The kiss was intense, and hot flushes of passion slowly invaded their bodies. Danny's grip grew tight, and she surrendered to his touch. She wildly ran her fingers through his hair. He whispered, "I'm really missing you. Come with me tonight."

She mildly pushed away. Directly facing him she said, "Danny, we have to talk."

"Yes," he said in a deep but soft, sensuous voice. Suddenly, from behind Danny came a loud voice.

"Hey, break it up you two."

A dull, cold chill ran through Laura's spine.

Julio Morales, the class clown, and unfortunately at this point and time Danny's best friend, interrupted. "I thought I'd find you here. We have track practice, remember? Or did that pretty girl of yours make you forget?"

Danny put his hands up against the locker. "Got to

hand it to you, buddy. You sure know how to spoil a great moment."

Julio put one arm up against the locker, "Hello, Laura, how are you?"

Laura answered coyishly, "I'm fine Julio. I'm just fine." She slowly began to come out of the clouds and back to reality.

"Julio, go on to practice. I'll meet you there."

Laura removed Danny's hand from her waist. "I think it's best that you leave now, Danny."

"Laura, we need to talk," he said.

A cold anger flashed across her face as she remembered why she was in this predicament in the first place. Danny tried to repeat the tender moment.

"No, don't come close to me," she said as she pushed him away. "I think it's best if we stayed away from each other."

A blank look of despair came upon Danny's face. "What are you talking about? A minute ago you were in my arms, and I could feel your love. You're becoming so hot and cold. What's up, baby?"

Laura blurted out desperately, "That kiss was a good-bye kiss."

Danny looked stunned, as if someone had slapped him.

"What? Are you telling me you want to see other guys? Is that it? Laura, I love you. You love me."

"Enough! I don't want to talk anymore. It's over, Dan. Get it through your head," she cried as she continued to take a few steps back, and tears slowly trickled down her face.

Laura walked away blindly; her eyes filled with tears. She firmly clutched her notebooks and quickly ran to the bathroom hoping no one would be around. As she looked in the mirror, she groaned out loud, "Oh, no. Now look at yourself, Laura. Your mascara is smeared. You look like a raccoon. Your eyes look horrible. Take a deep breath and calm down."

She washed her face and slowly dried her hands and proceeded to freshen her face with make-up. As she fumbled through her purse looking for her lipstick, Dan's letter fell to the floor.

She stooped down to pick it up, took a deep breath, and began reading it.

Dearest Laura,

I don't know why you are upset and don't want to talk with me on the phone. I hope it's nothing you heard about me. I really can't think of any other reason other than you are wanting to break up with me to see other people. We've never discussed it in the two years we've been going steady. I cannot think of any other reason. So, to make it easy on you, I will let you go. But you must know that for me you are the only one. I love you. I don't think you'll remember what today is or what it should have been. For what it's worth, today we were supposed to celebrate the two years you and I have been together. Take care. Gook luck.

Danny López

P.S. Here's another poem that I have written to you.

LAURA

As I walk the halls of

San Manuel High

I feel a tear drop fall from

My eye

My heart feels pain from

A feeling called sorrow

For it knows with you

There will be no tomorrow

If I could touch you

If I could once again kiss you

If I could know what troubles you deep in your heart

We would never be apart

For me there's no one but you

Please don't let it be true

Please don't say we're through

DANNY

Tears rolled down Laura's face as she remembered the many poems Danny had written to her in the past. In all her dismay, she had completely overlooked this special day, March 24. Laura gently hugged herself, closed her eyes, and thought of the first time they met. It was a fresh, rainy day; and they were freshmen in high school. Laura had been given the task, along with Aissa in her journalism class, to photograph the junior varsity football team which was in spring training for next year.

In retrospect, Laura vividly remembered the day. She recalled how she disapproved of jocks and their brainless, physical activities which she was sure they only performed to look good and to attract girls.

To top it off, this useless activity had a name. It was called football. How pathetic. Despite her persuasive argument, Mrs. De León insisted she take pictures as well as get a better understanding of the sport.

Laura dragged her feet all the way to the football stadium. Aissa was practically running. Her long legs made it even more difficult for Laura to keep up. By the time Laura reached the football field, Aissa had already received permission from the coach and was walking flirtatiously toward the middle of the field.

When Laura caught up with Aissa, she rolled her eyes back in disgust. Some of the football members focused their attention on Aissa.

"I can't believe these hoodlums act as if they have never seen a girl before."

"Laura, get over here!" yelled Aissa.

It was no wonder guys wanted to be in football. They seemed to get the same attention from other girls as they did from Aissa.

"Laura, this is Coach Ramos."

"Hello, Mr. Ramos."

Coach Ramos directed the girls, "Go ahead and take your shots, and make it quick. We have to get on with practice. Hey, Thomas..."

"You talking to me coach?" Thomas asked as he removed his gold and white helmet from his head.

"Throw the football to Danny on this next play," Coach Ramos ordered.

"Oh, hi, Aissa," said Julio, temporarily distracted.

"Hi, Julio."

"Okay, okay." interrupted Laura impatiently as she focused her camera and began shooting. "Let's just get this over with," she whispered to Aissa.

Laura walked farther up ahead to take a picture of Danny running for the ball while Aissa stayed back to photograph Thomas throwing the ball. As Laura took the picture, it seemed the ball was coming directly toward her and so was Danny.

"HEY! STOP!" yelled Laura.

Danny continued running, turning back toward Thomas, totally oblivious to Laura's words. He was intent on catching the ball.

Laura screamed as she felt Danny slam her to the ground. Laura lay flat for a moment and was out of breath. She thought she'd faint. The rest of the team laughed hilariously.

"Are you all right? I'm so sorry," said Danny as he took off his helmet and knelt down on one knee next to her.

"Is she all right?" yelled Aissa, running to Laura's side.

As Laura came to, she opened her eyes; and there was Danny.

"Here, let me help you get up."

"Get your grubby hands off me. I'm okay."

"I'm sorry. I really am," said Danny.

Aissa brushed the grass from Laura's blouse and jeans. "I picked up your camera. I think it's broken."

"I didn't see you with my helmet. Besides you should have been farther away from the field."

Laura looked numbed by the remark. "Are you implying that this is my fault, you jerk," she said with a half smile.

"Well, you were inside the field. You should have been on the side lines. What's your name?" he asked.

"Why do you want to know my name?" asked Laura, swept away by his emerald-green eyes; long, curly lashes; handsome face; creamy complexion; and black hair.

"So I can report you to the journalism teacher," he remarked jokingly.

Laura laughed loudly and was surprised at how safe he

made her feel. Yes, there was an instant attraction between the two. She could not help but notice how gallant he looked in his football uniform. From that moment on, Laura would see "jocks" from a different point of view.

That was the beginning of their relationship. Looking back, she wondered if she would do it again. She looked in the mirror of the girls' bathroom. Who would have thought it would end like this, pregnant at seventeen? She composed herself and put the letter back in her purse. Suddenly, an urge to eat rushed through her body. "Look at the time. Five o'clock. I missed debate practice. Thelma will be furious. It's too late now," she thought to herself.

CHAPTER SIX

"Laura," said Anna excitedly, "I thought you'd never get here. Relax, gosh! I've never seen you like this."

"Like what?" asked Laura.

"Like a dog, so excited because he's finally going to be fed."

"A dog! A dog! Are you comparing me to a dog?" cried Laura as she swatted Anna on her back with a purse.

"I haven't been eating correctly with this flu. I'm over it now, and I'm just trying to regain my weight. Where do you want to go have a snack?"

"Relax. It's only a joke, Laura. Let's go to Stars and have a Coke and fries," replied Anna.

Anna watched Laura in awe as she nearly swallowed her delicious, foot-long, chile hot dog and golden-brown onion rings.

"That's one small snack, Laura!" exclaimed Anna surprisingly. "Oh, Laura, be careful. You spilled a big blot of chile on your gorgeous, red blouse.

"Oh, no!" moaned Laura as she quickly took a napkin and wiped the stain from her blouse. "I hope it comes off. My mom paid $65 for this blouse, and it is one of the few that I feel comfortable wearing."

"Don't look now," said Anna excitedly.

"What?"

"Look who just parked in front of us."

Laura looked up, and Anna said, "Don't look. You're making it obvious."

"Daisy Tyler. So, what? If you've seen one tacky, bad, nasty girl, you've seen them all."

"I think that's a new guy she's with. Don't make it obvious, but can you see who she's with?"

Laura looked toward the other car and said, "I don't think it's anyone from our school."

"Well, of course, it wouldn't be anyone from our school. She's dated just about every guy," replied Anna with a devious look on her face.

"Look at how close they're sitting together. Watch how she keeps throwing her hair over her shoulder and that big, bright smile," she said enviously. "What type of signals is she sending out to this guy?" Anna continued as she slurped her last sip of the drink.

Laura swapped Anna on the shoulder, "Will you stop looking at them. She knows we're watching."

Anna grabbed the steering wheel tightly and sat bolt-upright. "Oh, goodness! Now they're kissing. Gosh! She has some nerve. The reputation she has in school definitely serves her. That goes for her best friend, María Guerra, too!"

Daisy tossed her long, blonde hair back and forth continuously and flashed sultry looks at her date. Her big, green eyes constantly turned toward the girls, making sure they were enveloped in her game.

Laura turned to Anna and remarked, "You know, with as many boys as Daisy and María have dated and the reputation they proudly flaunt, you'd think one of them would end up pregnant. But, of course not. I guess they know how to take care of themselves. They're not stupid and naive about sex."

"Ready to go?" asked Laura.

"Yes, we have that party tonight. I guess Daisy is starting early."

As Anna drove out of the driveway of Laura's house, Laura waved good-bye, "Have fun at the party tonight, Anna."

CHAPTER SEVEN

*A*nna looked in the mirror and added the finishing touches to her face. "Hmmm, beauty tips," she thought as she pressed the lipstick pencil to her lips and deftly outlined them. She continued with a fuschia-colored lipstick that gave her lips a supple look.

She turned to look at herself in a full-length mirror. Everything seemed perfect. Her full, lustrous hair dropped to her waist. The dangling earrings gave her a fun look. She had chosen an off-the-shoulder, pastel dress with a big bow on the back. It hugged her slim, curvy figure. The outfit looked perfect. The theme was a Hawaiian party.

"Come on in, Michelle," Mrs. Guzmán said sweetly.

"Mom, we don't have time. We have to go," remarked Anna.

"You look gorgeous, Michelle."

"Thank you, Mrs. Guzmán."

"Dad, we'll be home early," said Anna as she gently pushed Michelle to the door.

"Well, no drinking and say no to drugs, " Anna's mom called.

"Mom, don't be so silly," she said smiling.

As Michelle and Anna drove to the party, Anna hastily pulled out her compact mirror to look at herself one more time.

She looked toward Michelle.

"Michelle, you look great. That royal blue sure does become you."

"You like it? My mini-skirt isn't too short, is it?' she asked as she tried to pull her skirt down with one hand and keep the other on the wheel.

"Are you kidding! Mini-skirts are in. You know that. And your short-sleeved blouse with the low v-neck looks sexy. Okay, come on, out with it. Who are you trying to attract?" asked Michelle tauntingly.

"No one," replied Anna.

"Come on. I know you better than that. Who is it? Oh, I know, Kevin Barnes."

"Are you crazy? He's goofy looking."

"No, not at all. He's rather cute and intelligent."

"But he's kind of nerdy," replied Anna.

"He's not nerdy, and he looks really great in jeans."

"But, he's not a football player."

"So, what! I still noticed an attraction between you two in sixth-period class.

"He really does have a nice baby face, doesn't he?" said Anna in a tone that exposed her true feelings.

"Anna, is there something I should know?"

"Well, all right. I confess. This may sound dumb, but the truth is there is a strong attraction between Kevin and me.

However, my parents would never hear of it. My parents are prejudiced against white people. If my dad was to find out that I was dating a white boy, he'd probably have a heart attack and die. I'd probably be sent off to my aunt's home in California.

Michelle opened her eyes in surprise, causing her forehead furrows to show.

"Anna, I don't understand. I'm white. Michelle Jennings, that's my name. Don't they know that?"

"Oh, don't get me wrong. I can have a hundred white friends, but I'm not allowed to have a relationship with one of them."

As Michelle parked the car at San Manuel High's gym, she gently put her hand over Anna's shoulder, "I'm really sorry your parents feel that way."

"That's okay. Come on Michelle, let's go have fun. I don't want to talk about it. We'll talk later."

They were greeted at the entrance of the gym by the sophomore committee in charge of handing out a Hawaiian lei to place around their neck.

"Here is the finishing touch," said Andrea Walsh as she tucked orchids behind their ears.

"Now you girls really look Hawaiian," remarked Andrea as she flashed a smile that caused the dimple on her chin to appear. She was short and chubby, but her true personality always won her many friends. It was no accident when she was crowned band sweetheart.

The gym was magically transformed. As usual those creative, competitive sophomores had done a super job. The walls were covered with long, wide paintings of the beach; sea shells; and surfers attempting to ride the waves. The balloons gave it a touch of festive fun. At the far right corner were two people dressed as Hawaiians. "How did they persuade them to dress that way?" thought Anna.

The far left corner had a Hawaiian photographic setting for any students wishing to have their pictures taken. Anna watched as the sophomore class president, Briana Gómez, and vice president, Fidel Guerra, walked happily in their Hawaiian attire.

"These sophomores went all out, didn't they, Michelle?" Anna asked. "Well, you know, Anna, when it comes to competing with the junior and senior classes, these sophomores really do challenge us."

"I wonder what prom night will look like this year?" she said dreamily. Anna watched as the popular Briana Gómez and her clique—Fidel Guerra, Rayan Davis, Rachel Lang, Ricky Gómez and Pat Díaz—hurriedly went from station-to-station making sure everything was completed to the best of their ability. Anna smiled as she thought of her best friends when they were sophomores last year. They, too, had thrown a fine party. It was in October, so it was a Halloween theme.

"Hi, Anna," Briana waved hello.

"Hi, Michelle."

The girls waved back. "Hi, Briana. Hello, Fidel."

Michelle said cheerfully, "You guys did a great job!"

"Thank you. Well, you know us sophomores. We stop at nothing," remarked Fidel proudly.

Michelle touched Briana's Hawaiian, straw skirt. "Yes, I can tell. When you sophomores have a party, you really like to party!"

Briana had been blessed with the most exquisite qualities given to a young woman. Her curvy, slim figure stood at an even 5 feet 9 inches. Her silky, black, wavy hair complemented her almond-shaped, blue eyes and enhanced her high cheek bones and beautifully rounded lips. It was no secret why she was constantly winning beauty pageants.

"Well, I guess you'll be in the varsity cheerleading squad with us next year, huh, Briana?" asked Michelle.

Briana smiled confidently and said, "I sure hope so. But I am not counting my chickens before they're hatched."

Anna tapped Briana delicately on her shoulder and whispered, "Don't forget to vote for me for head cheerleader next year."

"Yes, of course," said Briana as she and her friends waved good-bye and walked away."

Michelle and Anna's hips began swaying to the music. Anna jumped with excitement and said, "Oh, I love that song, 'True Friends Will Never Let You Down.'"

Michelle grabbed Anna's arm. "Hey look. There's Julio, Danny, Thomas, oh, and Kevin."

"Anna, don't freak out; but they're coming this way."

Anna's heart began to race; her legs felt faint. Not even in the worst pressure during cheerleading tryouts had she ever experienced such nervous feelings. She tried to catch her breath.

"Hello, Anna. Hi, Michelle."

"Hi Danny, Julio, Thomas, and Kevin," replied the girls as smiles and handshakes were exchanged.

Danny asked, "Anna, is Laura coming?"

Anna cuffed her hand to her ear, "What did you say Danny?"

Danny ran his fingers through his hair and asked again, "I said, is Laura coming to the dance?"

"No. She said she isn't feeling too well."

"What do you mean, she isn't feeling too well? Oh, I don't know what is going on with Laura. She sure has been acting strange these last few weeks. What do you think is wrong, Anna?"

Anna was trying hard to sympathize with Danny but really wanted to talk to Kevin. She tried to finish the conversation as quickly as possible.

Julio grabbed Michelle's hand, "Let's go dance."

As Michelle and Julio walked to the dance floor, the circle became smaller. Kevin was now next to Anna. Kevin looked around nervously, not wanting to interrupt Danny and Anna's conversation. Anna wished desperately that he would.

Danny wanted answers. "Anna, so what do think?"

Anna crossed her arms. "What? Danny, you got me; you're her boyfriend."

"Not anymore. She doesn't want to have anything to do with me. I don't know what I've done that's so wrong."

Anna looked up to Danny and said with compassion, "I really wish I could tell you, but she's not sharing any secrets with me these days."

The song ended, and the D.J. moved to a slower pace. A quiet, nervous cough came from Kevin as he lightly tapped Anna on her shoulder. "Anna, would you like to dance?"

Anna gazed shyly into Kevin's clear, blue eyes. "Yes."

Michelle flashed a thumbs-up to Anna as she walked onto the dance floor. Anna was sure Kevin had seen that and could feel her face blushing. Kevin bent down, kissed her upturned palms, and gently wrapped his arms around Anna's small waist. He looked at the sweet, ivory, oval shape of her face, circled in her walnut-brown hair, and dropped his head down close to Anna's shoulder. Anna wrapped her arms around his neck, and the slow dance began. For a while only silence followed. Finally, he gently whispered. "You look really pretty in that dress, Anna."

"Thank you, Kevin. You look nice in your western shirt."

"Thanks. Well, you know how us nerds love cattle ranching."

Anna pulled away from him, trying hard to relieve her dry mouth. "I never said you were a nerd."

Kevin's smile mesmerized her as she extended her arms a little and looked up to talk to him.

"Danny said that Laura told him that's what you thought about me." Kevin confidently threw his head back. "I guess the popular girl that you are, cheerleader and all, you're probably not interested in a nerdy cowboy like me."

"I never said that." Anna felt jittery.

"So, what are you saying?" he asked, brushing his fingers though his hair. He pushed away from her.

"Anna, would you go out with me?"

Anna was startled by his question but replied softly, "Sure, Kevin, I would like to go out with you sometime."

They stood for a while not moving to the music. For a split second no one seemed to dance around them. Kevin could not believe he was actually having this conversation with a girl he'd had a crush on for more than a year. Anna could hardly stand it. Then his handsome smile made her smile and relax. She sank into his arms but quickly pulled back.

"It's just that my parents wouldn't understand."

"What about your parents? Daddy's girl?"

The two laughed as they hugged and continued dancing. The next dance was another slow tune. Anna felt safe in Kevin's embrace. She rested her head on his shoulder, and in that moment Anna realized she was falling in love with Kevin Barnes. Kevin wished the slow dance would never end. Anna's soft hair smelled of roses. He closed his eyes and danced contently to the music. And then, magically, their lips met. Kevin was convinced the girl he'd had a crush on for so long felt the same way he did.

Michelle looked down at her watch and realized that despite the fun they were having, the hour was quickly growing late. The girls walked outside, opened the doors to the car, and waved good-bye to Kevin and the gang.

"Oh, Michelle!" yelled Anna, hardly restraining herself. "He is a dream, an absolute dream. We kissed on the dance floor."

"I know. I saw you, and so did the rest of San Manuel High."

"Michelle, did you kiss Fidel?" asked Anna as they both burst out laughing.

"I'm not telling. What are you going to do about you and Kevin?"

"Well, I'm not sure," said Anna with a confused look on her face. "I know I can trust my mom." She took a deep breath, "and as for my dad, I'll just tell him we're simply good friends."

"Yeah," smiled Michelle, "really good friends. If anything happens, if...if it gets more serious, what will you do?"

"I don't know. There are so many places I'd like to go. I really don't have time for a serious relationship."

Michelle was stunned by Anna's answer. "Are you serious? Any girl would die to be in your shoes!"

Anna twirled her hair. "He is extremely good looking; and as I said, I'll tackle that problem if we ever get there."

CHAPTER EIGHT

The morning sun crept into Laura's bedroom. She slowly sat on her bed and grabbed the cracker box from under it. She had read in the pamphlet that crackers were good for settling your stomach. "Oh my goodness," she groaned as she bent over to hide the pregnancy information given to her from a nurse in a local clinic. There were also other forms of literature Laura took from the clinic. "I have to hide all of these pamphlets," she thought as she threw some of them into the trash can. "No, I can't do that," she thought. "Mom may find them." She quickly tucked them away in her notebook. "There that's better. When I get to school, I'll dispose of them."

Laura had read the pamphlets on pregnancy over the weekend and many of her questions had been answered, such as why was she happy one moment and in tears the next? Why would she cry over something as simple as the siren of an ambulance? Why were her breasts extremely tender and looking slightly larger?

She learned to conceal her body changes so well that no one—not her parents, friends or relatives—suspected she was pregnant. She knew she had to make a decision as soon as possible.

Laura called and went to an agency that specialized in motherhood. She did not dare identify herself. She was given some choices. Terminating the pregnancy before the first trimester was one choice. Another was putting the baby up for adoption. Keeping the baby would be the most difficult choice; for, she was told, it would change her entire life. However, there were programs to help pregnant teens. She was now ending her first trimester. She would have to make her choice.

Laura was locking the door to her house when Anna drove into the driveway.

"Well, do you feel better now?" Anna questioned. "You didn't return my calls this week."

"I'm better now, ...so," Laura put the last piece of toast in her mouth.

"So what?" Anna knew Laura wanted to know about the party.

"So, tell me about the weekend," inquired Laura anxiously.

"Hmmm... Where should I start? Rene Torres and Terry Houston walked into the hall as if they were in love. They were holding hands. Looking at them, you'd think they were in love forever."

"Get out of here!" remarked Laura smiling.

Anna carefully turned the stirring wheel to her car as she continued to drive. Her face looked as if it would explode if she didn't tell her best friend the entire gossip of the night before. "Would you believe he had his arms wrapped around her waist so tight, I'm not sure how she could breathe." Laura gently hit Anna across her shoulder and smiled.

"Come on."

"I'm serious. She was wearing a tight, red dress." Anna

squinted her eyes and flashed a pitiful look at Laura. "You should have seen the look on Nancy Rutledge's face."

Laura cuffed her hands to her mouth and muffled, "Poor Nancy."

Anna continued, "We thought she'd faint."

"Two days after breaking up and he is already with another girl."

"What a jerk."

"What did Nancy do?"

"Nancy danced the night away and pretended that it did not bother her."

"Good for her. What else?" Laura wanted to hear about Danny.

"Well, I guess I'll tell you now."

As they drove up to the parking lot at San Manuel High and stepped out of the car, Laura's curiosity got the best of her. "What? What?" she asked as she jumped up and down like a girl who'd just won first prize.

"Laura," she said looking straight into her eyes, "Kevin and I are going steady."

Laura's eyes danced with joy, "That's wonderful! When? How? Where did this happen? Why didn't you call me?" she questioned out of breath.

Anna looked at Laura with a silly look on her face. "I tried Laura. You wouldn't return my calls, remember? Anyway, it happened at the Hawaiian dance this last weekend. He is a real gentleman."

"But, but what about your parents?"

"What about them? Oh, yes. I spoke to Mom over the weekend. She trusts my judgment. Her face beamed with excitement as I told her about the dance."

"What about your dad?"

"My dad will only know that we are friends...period. If the relationship evolves into a more serious one, then he'll have to know. Simple as that."

As the girls neared their lockers, Anna's hand covered her forehead. "Oh my goodness. I almost forgot. Laura, everyone asked for you." Anna raised her right eyebrow. "Someone was really concerned."

Laura put her head down because she knew what Anna was going to say.

"Laura, Danny is concerned. Please talk to him, and get it over with."

Laura felt relieved to hear he was still interested in her.

"Don't worry. He wasn't dancing with anyone. Please talk to him."

"I think he suspects I'm lying to him." Laura put her books into her locker and took her first-period books out.

"Oh, and guess what else? Fidel Mares asked Michelle Smith to go steady."

Laura looked stunned as she tried to take in all the news Anna seemed to be pouring out. "I really missed a lot not going to the party."

"Well, we're both going to miss even more if we don't run to first period. See yah!" yelled Anna.

"Laura, wait up!" yelled a familiar, timid voice behind Laura.

Laura grabbed the strap from her brown purse and put it over her shoulder.

"Hi, Nancy. My, it's been so long."

"Yes, I know," said Nancy nervously as she tossed her blond hair back.

"Listen, I was wondering. Do you have time to talk after school?"

Laura sighed and felt obliged to meet her after school if she needed to talk. They both walked briskly to classes.

"Why sure. Is everything all right? Wait a minute. Did your brother flush your favorite earrings down the toilet?" asked Laura, hoping to have Nancy smile. Nancy ignored the joke.

"You heard about the breakup between Rene and me?"

"Yes, I'm sorry. But cheer up. You're so pretty. It's silly sticking to one guy. Listen, Nancy. We have less than a minute to make it to class before the tardy bell rings," Laura said, looking at her watch.

Nancy yelled as she ran to class, "Laura, I'll meet you here at the locker after school."

CHAPTER NINE

*N*ancy stood waiting anxiously by Laura's locker, holding her books tightly to her chest. She hugged them so tightly, she could feel her arms beginning to hurt.

"Well, how were your classes today, Laura?"

Laura let out a sigh of relief as she opened the combination lock and threw her books inside. She tiredly rubbed her eyes.

"We had a test in chemistry today. I think I blew it."

Nancy looked at Laura with a sweet but sympathetic look.

"Well, maybe Mr. Brock will give your class a big curve if the rest of the class bombed."

Laura flashed half a grin; her eyes looked wishful. "I don't think I'll be so lucky."

"He is super strict when it comes to tests. You know what his big motto is." The girls looked at each other and repeated Mr. Brook's motto: "Hard work and determination never come easy; but once you achieve it, success is sweet!"

As Laura and Nancy walked past the lockers and out the front doors of San Manuel High, Terry and Rene walked by. The look on Terry's face was that of victory. Nancy's heart began to pound quickly; she felt so embarrassed. Rene turned his face as if he were disgusted to have done what he did.

Laura turned to Nancy and said, "Ignore them, Nancy. Before you know it, he'll break up with her and go on to another girl."

The girls walked outside to find a bench to sit on. Nancy's face grew dim. She burst into tears.

Laura felt helpless. "Nancy, please, don't cry," she said softly as her arms swung around her for support. Nancy put her hands over her face.

"Oh, Laura, I've been such a fool. I should have known. I feel so cheap and used."

"Nancy, so many couples go through this. I mean, that's the way you know when it's the right relationship. You have to experience these things to grow from it."

"I've been so stupid," continued Nancy. "I'd heard about his flirting from my very own sister Karen. I was so blind! He treated me badly, but I kept loving him. He even kept me from you and Anna, my two good friends. I did it to make him happy," she replied as she stomped her feet on the ground. With a shaky voice, she continued with tears falling from her eyes. "I feel humiliated. But you know, Laura, the saddest thing about this is that if he called me to go out with him tonight, I probably would. I still miss him and love him so much. We've been together so long." She wiped the tears from her face.

"Nancy, it's not the end of the world. I know it's hard, but it will get better," said Laura. She tried to hold her tears back, thinking about her dilemma with Danny. Laura pulled Nancy's hair back.

"You've been hurt, but you'll get over him. Remember Anna's date, David, in the ninth grade? He broke up with her. Remember?" continued Laura holding Nancy's hand. "Remember when you and I both comforted her and told her it was going to be okay. Anna said she'd never find another like him. She said she'd never date again."

Laura looked straight into Nancy's eyes, "Where is Anna now? David is a big joke in her past. She wonders how she could have ever dated him."

Nancy burst out laughing with tears still stinging her face. "Yeah, I remember. When he tried to come back, she treated him like a piece of used candy and dumped him."

"You're right," said Laura. "She cried for days; and when we talked to her the following week, she was dating Randy Liberman." Laura smiled at Nancy, "You're going to be fine, silly. It will take a while, maybe a day or so," said Laura jokingly.

Nancy bit her bottom lip. "Yeah, you're right. I'm embarrassed that he is dating someone else. I think that's what hurts the most."

Nancy put her hand over her mouth and said, "Everyone in school knows."

"Well, Terry has herself a real winner," said Laura sarcastically. Nancy giggled. Laura reached over and hugged her.

"You're going to be just fine," she repeated as she gave Nancy a pat on her back. Nancy wiped the final tear from her face.

"It's getting late."

Nancy stood up and sighed a sigh of relief. "I feel better, Laura. Would you like for me to give you a ride home?"

"That would be nice," replied Laura.

"Let's walk over by the gym, so I can tell Anna."

The girls walked slowly to the parking lot.

"Hey, Nancy," said Laura as she opened the car door to Nancy's car, "what about a bite to eat?"

"How about a bite to eat?" Nancy replied quickly. "That's not a bad idea. Where at?"

"El Rey restaurant. Thelma Muñoz works there. We were supposed to meet for debate practice. She didn't show."

Nancy parked the car alongside the boys' gym.

"This won't take long. I'll tell Anna to meet us at El Rey."

Laura walked in the gym and found Anna. She signaled for her to come over. Anna walked slowly.

"What's up?" asked Anna. She was dressed in school-color gym attire.

"Nancy and I are going to have a bite to eat at El Rey restaurant. Care to meet us there?"

"That sounds great," remarked Anna, leaning against the gym wall, "except I have a test tomorrow. I'll probably have to pass for today," she said smiling. Then Anna's face displayed concern, "How is Nancy doing?"

Laura pulled her blouse out and away from her body, "She's going to be okay."

Anna wiped the sweat from her face, "That's good. I'll give you a call later tonight."

Laura waved good-bye, "All right."

As Laura turned to exit the gym, Danny approached her. Shock and fear ran through Laura's surprised body.

"Hi, Laura," he said in a deep, sweet, calm voice.

"Hi Danny," she replied, looking down.

Danny grabbed Laura's shoulders and brought her closer to him. "Look at me, Laura. I don't know how to say this...." He took a deep breath. Laura stood motionless, lost in his grasp. Danny's gold and white gym clothes accented his manly features.

"I dream of you at night. I think of you during the day. My grades are going down. I can't concentrate well. If you are not seeing someone else, what is it? I can't do this anymore. Let's just call it off. I'm tired of this."

Danny put his arm around Laura's neck. He was drenched with sweat. Laura didn't notice. "Please, Laura, just tell me."

Laura felt her eyes beginning to sting. Tears tumbled down from her eyes.

"Tell me why you don't feel love for me anymore. What have I done?"

Laura tried to get away from his grip. "I'm not, I'm not

ready to talk about it."

"About what? You're driving me crazy. I thought I was your best friend. Do you have cancer, a brain tumor...or what?"

"No. No, it's nothing like that," she said smiling. She wiped the tears from her eyes.

"Can I see you tonight, Laura?"

"Ah, yeah. I think it's a good idea. I'll call you, so you can come over."

"Laura, I know what is going on. You're making plans to move on. Well that's just fine with me," he said proudly.

"Hey, Dan," yelled Julio. "The coach is looking for you."

"I'll be right there."

Laura tried to walk away.

"Is it truly over between us? Yes, of course, I should have known. That's what you wanted all along."

Laura turned and put her hand over his mouth. "What's wrong with you? Shhh...shhh, please keep your voice down," she said, embarrassed. She noticed some of the cheering squad beginning to take notice.

He grabbed her upper arm and drew her toward him. He began yelling like a mad man, "So that's what you want! It's over! So you can date other guys! I guess I'll start dating as well. Maybe I'll start with some of your friends. No wait," he continued pulling her closer to him. "Maybe you'd like to see me with Daisy or someone from that crowd."

Laura pulled away. "You don't understand anything, you jerk!" she yelled as tears begin to sting her eyes. "Just leave me alone; and never, ever talk to me again." Laura felt as if she would burst and faint.

"Laura, if I don't understand, then tell me." He tightened his lips in exasperation.

"Okay," she said firmly, "you're right. It is time to share my secret." Laura walked away as fast as she could. As she neared Nancy's car, she quickly dried her tears. She realized in her heart the time was nearing, and this secret she had kept all to herself had to be revealed. The torture she felt had to be released.

Nancy honked for Laura to hurry. As she opened the car door to get in, Nancy quickly asked, "I saw him walking into the gym. What happened?"

"Nothing happened."

Nancy gently patted Laura's knee. "A while ago I was crying. Come on. You can't fool me. I know you talked. I saw you." Nancy smiled, "That's funny. Rene and I break up, and you and Danny get back together."

"We're not getting back together."

"What's wrong with you?" asked Nancy as they drove off. "Everyone knows you both were made for each other. He is so sweet and good looking, intelligent, with a sure future. The whole time you two have been apart, he has not looked at another girl."

Laura looked at Nancy and tried to change the subject.

"For a girl who was in tears and extremely depressed only fifteen minutes ago, you sure have changed. What was the reason Rene broke up with you?"

Nancy thought for a while. She changed the radio station. "Well, you know. Hmmm, there were a lot of reasons."

Laura put her fingers to her mouth. "Was there one in particular?" Laura made a fist and gently tapped Nancy on the shoulder. She hoped having Nancy talk about it would make her feel better. Nancy felt embarrassed.

"Well, do you really want to know?"

Laura's face looked concerned. "Of course I do. I'm asking, aren't I," she said mockingly.

"I think the biggest reason was because I wouldn't go all the way with him."

Laura's eyes opened wide. She was breathless and surprised. Her body shifted in the seat.

"What a jerk! Is that all?"

Nancy reached to change the radio station again. "I don't want to talk about it. Let's listen to the music."

Laura could see the betrayal of Rene's breakup beginning to surface on Nancy's face. "Good idea," said Laura as the thought still clung to her mind. She thought, "If I had just said no the first time, it would have been all right. Would he have left me?" she wondered. "I guess I'll never know. It's too late to think about that now." Laura tried to forget her dilemma.

Nancy pulled into El Rey Restaurant and parked. "Well, we're here. Let's get out. I'm starving."

CHAPTER TEN

Julio stood with a towel wrapped around his waist. His dark brown hair was wet and falling to his forehead. "Hey, Dan, what's the big deal? You haven't been running well at practice." Julio snapped Dan with the tip of the towel. "What's on your mind, buddy? It's Laura, isn't it?" he answered his own question.

Dan tiredly removed his shoes and looked up at Julio, frustrated. "Ah, I don't know. I have a lot on my mind—Laura, exams, S.A.T. scores. Laura refuses to have anything to do with me. But that's not all that's bothering me," he replied with a smirk on his face.

"I noticed Rhonda Lee smiling at you," said Julio teasingly.

"Oh, come on. She is a friendly girl. She's only trying to be nice."

"Oh, yeah, sure," said Julio obnoxiously. He imitated her in a flirtatious, high-pitched voice.

"Hey, Danny, how are you doing?" He posed like a woman. "I notice you had a hard time answering Mrs. Girling's questions in geometry class. Do you need any help?"

Danny laughed loudly as the rest of the guys joined in the teasing remarks. "Yeah, yeah, get out of here," he replied as he walked into the shower. "Besides, I'm supposed to meet with Laura tonight."

"Wuu-uuz..." came the teasing sounds from male voices. "That means you'll probably get back together, huh, dude?"

Danny stuck his head out of the shower, "More like, break up forever."

CHAPTER ELEVEN

A cool breeze filled the night. The stars were like numerous diamonds scattered across an immense, dark wall. They sparkled like glitter. The contrast of night and stars was extraordinarily beautiful. Danny stepped out of his red Mustang and walked up to Laura's front porch. As he rang the door bell, he wiped the sweat from his hands. He was nervous.

"Hello, Mrs. Garza. Is Laura here?"

Mrs. Garza's face smiled with delight. "Yes, she is getting dressed. Come in. Come in. I haven't seen you in a while. It's good to see you again." She swung her arms around Danny and embraced him. Danny hadn't visited them for a while. He felt like a stranger.

"Thank you."

"Here, take a seat." She picked up the scattered pages of the newspaper from the sofa to give him room to sit.

"Won't you sit down?"

"No, that's okay, I'll just...."

"Hi, Danny," interrupted Laura, not giving him time to finish his sentence. Laura pulled her blue, cotton blouse away from her stomach.

"Mom, I'll be home early."

"Where are you all going?"

"Probably Manny's restaurant," answered Laura.

"We'll see ya later, Mrs. Garza. It was good talking to you again."

"You all drive safely. Tomorrow is a school day, so be back early," called Mrs. Garza as they drove off.

Danny could feel his palms beginning to sweat against the steering wheel. "Is the air conditioning too cold?" he asked sweetly.

No, no, it's just fine," she replied. Her hands were crossed, and she moved her legs to a crossed position. Danny wiped his palms on his jeans.

"Would you like to go have dinner?"

"No, I'm not hungry," Laura replied hesitantly. "Let's just go to Marshal Land Park where it's nice and quiet, and we can talk."

Danny parked the car and rolled the window down.

"Danny, I think we'd better get out for what I'm about to tell you."

Danny's face looked full of curiosity. As Laura stepped out of the car, she took a deep breath hoping she could relieve the pressure that had mounted due to this inevitable talk. Laura lifted herself up on a concrete table and prepared herself to speak. She tossed her hair back and pulled her blouse away from her stomach.

"Danny, I don't know how to tell you this," she began. "It's been two-and-a-half months, and we're about to finish our junior year. I don't know how this happened," she began to speak nervously and quickly. "Well, I know how it happened; but I can't believe it happened to me, to us. I had so many plans for the future."

Danny put his hands on Laura's shoulder, "Slow down, what are you trying to tell me?"

"Danny, I've ruined your life and mine," she continued with tears running down her face. "I'm sorry. I'm...I'm pregnant."

Danny's face turned white. The news of her pregnancy seemed to slap him in the face.

Laura looked Danny straight in the eyes, "Yes, Danny, you heard right," she said with a shaky voice. "I'm pregnant. I feel so trapped. I haven't talked to a single soul. That's why I couldn't face you. I was so angry with you." She pounded him on the chest, "You said everything would be all right. You'd take care of me.... Well, what now, Mr. Know It All?"

The situation was getting out-of-hand. Danny stood motionless, letting Laura hit him, stunned by the news he'd just heard. Laura pushed him away.

"I've been wearing these ridiculous shirts because I feel fat. Look at me. My breasts have grown, and I vomit just about every morning. I feel awful, just awful. I feel guilty. I've let everyone down. My parents...how am I going to tell my parents?" She looked at him angrily. "What about our scholarships? What about those dreams?" she yelled out-of-control.

Danny walked over to Laura and wrapped his arms around her. He stroked her hair, "Shh shh, calm down, Laura. It's going to be all right," he whispered.

Laura, once again, angrily pushed way from him. "Calm down? Calm down? The last time you told me everything would be okay, I got pregnant."

"Laura, please, I'll think of something."

Danny was desperate to find a solution to the problem. He felt as scared and trapped as Laura but had to be strong in order to calm Laura down. Laura's frustrations over the last months had finally surfaced. Her tears and fears of the reality of being pregnant were finally being shared by the very person who helped put her in this predicament.

"I've been through so much these last months," she said, still crying.

"Why didn't you tell me before?" asked Danny calmly.

"I couldn't tell you!" she yelled, crying.

"I'd run the risk of the whole school finding out—my teachers, my relatives, your family."

Laura put her hands over her face in shame. Danny came to her aid. Laura walked away from him giving him a gesture to stay away. As she wiped the tears from her eyes, she said, "Danny, I can only think of one solution for this situation. I think...I think the answer is to have an abortion."

"What?" questioned Danny in a shaking voice.

Laura turned to Danny, "We'll lose our chances for the scholarship next year, and our families would be so disappointed in us."

"Laura, I'll stand by whatever decision you make. But I don't think you've weighed the options very carefully."

"Oh, so what are you saying Danny?" she retorted angrily. "That I keep the baby, drop out of school, and live with my parents? Get a job at the local Wal-Mart and accept my fate because of one stupid careless mistake?" she responded hysterically.

"I'm not saying that Laura."

"Well, then what.... what!" she yelled, crying out-of-control.

"Laura, get a hold of yourself, please."

"No, YOU get a hold of yourself. You're not the one that's pregnant. I am. You're not the one the students are going to laugh and talk about. I am. You aren't the one whose whole life was turned upside down in a matter of days. I should have known better. I just didn't think it would happen to me. Danny, I'm so scared. I'm so scared. Please help me."

Laura slowly sat on the ground. She curled up in a fetal position, and Danny tried to comfort her. Her crying voice became desperate. Danny wrapped his arms around her and stood motionless, still in shock and with no answers. Laura continued weeping. As the tears became less, Laura calmed down. Danny then sat her on the bench and squatted down in front of her. He took her hands and cupped them inside of his.

"Laura, I don't know what to do about this. But I feel we should talk to someone else before we make a decision. Maybe there are other options."

"Like what, Danny, adoption? I can't do that. I'd feel so guilty knowing my own baby is out there somewhere."

"I don't know what options, Laura. Maybe if we spoke to a counselor, he could tell us; and we'd make the best decision for us."

Laura hugged Danny; and for the first time since her pregnancy, she felt as if a big rock had been lifted from her shoulders.

"I'm glad you told me, Laura."

She whispered to Danny, "I should have told you a lot sooner."

They stood up, locked in each other's arms. Laura was swept into a dreamy state of mind as Danny moved closer, towering over her. Laura wrapped her arms around his neck. Danny clasped his arms around her waist.

"Danny," she said as she pulled back to look at him, "I was angry and said stupid things. I'm not the type of girl that could terminate a pregnancy and go on through life thinking nothing about the situation. I know maybe other girls would, and for them it's the right decision. But I personally would not feel right about it. Remember the rumors last year about Sophie Reyes being pregnant by Charlie Lerma? She terminated her pregnancy and bragged about it too. She didn't think anything about it; and I hear she's is in college now, happy about her decision. You know, I read in an article that every day over 2,700 girls get pregnant in the United States; and half terminate the pregnancy. And 43 percent of sexually active girls become pregnant before the age of twenty. Seventy percent of teenage mothers are unmarried.

"Wow, that many? " replied Danny.

Laura continued to recite the information she'd memo-
rized. "Forty-four percent of teenage mothers drop out of high
school. Babies born to girls under twenty will have more health
problems and will do worse in school than babies born to
women over twenty. Statistics show that 90 percent of teenage
marriages end in divorce. I know it's not the best move for my
career. Many girls in my situation would terminate the pregnancy. I just can't do that."

Laura hugged Danny again and took a deep, relaxing
breath. She felt the breeze against her face. The bright stars lit
up the sky like bursting fireworks creating brightly colored
light.

"I don't know how I'm going to do it, Danny."

Danny quickly interrupted Laura and put his middle
fingers over her mouth, "You mean, you don't know how we're
going to do it. I want to be involved 100 percent. I told you I'll
stand by you 100 percent. I really mean it. I love you so much."

As they continued embracing, Danny bent his head
down and locked his lips on Laura's. It felt as if they had not
seen each other for years. Suddenly, for a moment, everything
seemed back to normal. Laura felt secure, and Danny felt reassured. Without any words, their love for each other was rekin-
dled. Except now, the bond seemed much deeper.

CHAPTER TWELVE

*D*anny laid in his bed, fatigued, almost in a trance, with his eyes wide open. Each passing moment made him realize the severity of his mistake. He thought of his mistake. He thought of his plans for the future that would now take a drastic turn, possibly for the worse. He closed his eyes in disappointment. Yet he knew, no matter what, he would stand by Laura. If he decided to have nothing to do with her, he'd feel like a jerk. There was no way out of this.

He began to think how his parents would take the news, how disappointed they would be. Should he tell them himself or with Laura? Should he be with Laura when she tells her parents? What about school? Did it mean he'd sit out of the football and basketball teams his senior year? Danny turned over on his side and tried to get some sleep. The effort proved useless. Danny was unable to sleep the entire night.

A loud knock came from Danny's bedroom door.

"It's time to get up, or you'll be late for school," said his mother.

"Okay, I'm getting up," he replied in a groggy voice. Danny looked out the window. "Oh, gosh. Oh, wonderful," he thought. "Of course, it would be a foggy morning. It would definitely go with the way my life seems to be going at this point—dim and uncertain, which way to go?"

Driving his car to pick up Laura gave him a sense of relief. At least something was back in order in his life. Laura waited anxiously by the door. She peeked through the window and waited impatiently for Danny to drive up the driveway. "He's here," she thought, as she opened the front door.

"It's Danny, Mom."

"Oh," she said in a pleasant voice, "well that's sweet you two are back together."

"Yes, Mom," said Laura, not wanting to give her a chance to ask too many questions. "Good-bye."

She quickly ran to the car. She did not wait for Danny's usual walk up to the door. She didn't want to give her mother a chance to ask questions.

Laura wore a loose, polka-dot, navy-blue blouse with matching stirrup pants. Danny quickly looked at Laura up and down. "She doesn't look pregnant," he thought. Her breasts seemed larger, but her stomach didn't protrude like most pregnant women.

"Hello, Danny," she said warmly.

"Hi. Ready for school?"

"Yes."

As Danny turned the corner, he gave out a lazy yawn.

"I take it you didn't get much sleep."

"No, I didn't get any sleep last night. How about you?" he asked.

"This is one of the first nights I've really been able to

sleep. I was thinking maybe it's because I finally talked to you. I feel truly relaxed today, Danny," she said as she gave him a kiss on the cheek.

Danny welcomed the kiss with a smile. He continued driving carefully.

"Laura?"

"Yes," she answered as she lovingly kept her arms around him.

"Have you considered with whom we should talk?"

Laura quickly took her arms from around his shoulders. It seemed as if the words had hit a cord in her heart that brought her back to reality.

"Well, I've thought of a number of people; but I've narrowed it down."

"Who?" questioned Danny.

"I feel the people at the pregnancy clinic would be the most educated about these matters. That's where I went to pick up pamphlets about pregnancy and the different choices," she said embarrassingly. "I needed to find out information, and I couldn't ask anyone. So I felt it was the best place."

CHAPTER THIRTEEN

*D*anny parked his shiny, red sports car in the parking lot of San Manuel High. He walked around the car to the passenger's seat and opened the door for Laura. He gently took Laura's hand. Little was said as the two entered the front doors of the school.

"Listen, Laura, no matter what happens or what you choose, I will stand by you. I said it before, and I'll say it again. I mean it, and I promise. I don't know where this will take us. I don't know how this will affect our lives, but I'm willing to accept responsibility for my mistakes." Danny's speech sounded rehearsed as if he'd said it over and over in an effort to convince himself.

Laura looked at him, "You mean our mistakes." Danny felt a shiver run through his body. Yet as scared as he was, he would never let Laura know. As Danny and Laura walked through the halls of San Manuel High, Danny realized his life had changed drastically; and it would never be the same again from this moment on. Suddenly, walking through the halls seemed gloomy.

"Hey, buddy," said Julio, slapping Danny on his back. Julio flashed a thumbs up. His straight, jet black hair came down to his neck. "I heard and saw the good news. You and your girl are back together. That's cool, dude!" He tossed his head to keep the hair out of his face.

"Oh, yeah." Danny shook his head hesitantly.

"What do you mean by, oh, yeah? What about a smile?" Julio extended his hand, and a manly handshake was exchanged.

"Yeah, yeah," said Danny as he went through the motion of a unique handshake.

"I take it you'll be a lot happier in school and probably do better in sports. I have to get to class. I'll see you last period," said Julio.

"Hey, what are you talking about?" yelled Danny.

"Last period is athletics. We're in the same class together. Hello. Are you okay, Danny? Wow, you really are out of it. You are really distant, dude."

"Hey, Laura," said Anna.

Laura smiled and quickly took her books out of her locker and remarked, "Hi, Anna."

Anna closed her locker door and smiled at Laura. "Laura, you—there's something about you. You seem so pretty, a glow on your face. You look so lovely."

Laura rolled her eyes, "Oh, yeah, right."

"I heard the news." Anna fumbled with her books.

Laura switched her purse from one shoulder to the other. "My goodness! Word really travels fast!"

"Gosh, Laura, if I didn't know any better, I'd say you're relieved. You and Danny finally talked it out."

"What are you saying?" asked Laura, scratching the top of her head.

"Well, you seem happy. You're back to normal. You're smiling, telling jokes; your spirit is back; your cheeks seem rosy."

Laura blushed.

"You're even blushing."

Laura could not help herself. Ever since she told Danny about her problem, she felt so much better.

"Come on. I'll walk you to class. Oh, are you going home with me today, or will you be going home with Danny?"

Laura gave Anna a push. "Oh, come on. I'm going home with you."

"Hey great! Afterwards we'll go to El Rey restaurant."

"Wait," said Laura, "I almost forgot. I can't go home with you." Laura bit her fingernails. "Danny and I need to talk about something. I'll go home with you tomorrow," she said absentmindedly.

Anna bit her lip then smiled. "Well, I'm not coming to school tomorrow."

Laura look confused. "Why not?"

Anna crossed her arms. "Because it will be Saturday, you goober!"

Laura laughed out loud, "Oh, where is my mind today?" she asked as she kept walking down the hall and waving to friends as they walked to class.

"Well, I'll see you Monday."

Sitting on the bench reading her library book, Laura

waited patiently for Danny. She was suddenly blinded by two hands over her eyes. By the sweaty feel on the large palms of the hands, she knew it was a boy who was either extremely nervous or sweating badly.

"Danny?"

"How did you know it was me?"

"Your sweaty palms gave it away. Are you nervous or still sweating?"

Danny dried his palms on his pants and replied, "I'd say a little of both."

As the two walked hand-in-hand toward the car, a feeling of uncertainty ran through Laura's mind. Laura jerked her hand away from Danny.

"What's wrong, Laura?"

"I just don't feel right. I'm scared."

Danny quickly but gently grabbed her arm and towered over her. "Look, I know you're scared. I'm scared too, but I'm sure there's a way out. We're going to be all right. We're going to make it. We'll be one of those super couples that will juggle school, a job, and a baby," he said reassuring her. "We're not the first couple that's been down this road."

Laura was nervous. Danny's remark was not comforting.

"That's just what I mean. I'm not so sure I want to be a couple. Do you realize what will have to be done if we become a couple?"

"Yes, Laura," replied Danny, quietly looking down.

"Look at me, Danny!" she demanded.

Danny slowly lifted his head and focused his eyes on hers.

"Married, Danny. We'd have to get married," she said as tears began to well up in her eyes. "I'm not so sure I'm ready for that. Why make two mistakes?"

Danny put his hands in his jean pockets and said, "I've been thinking about that, Laura. Maybe you can live with me at my house."

"Or maybe we can live with my parents," said Laura quickly.

"No, wait a minute. I can't."

They both looked at each other.

"Laura, please don't cry. Oh, God, I wish this would have never happened. I'm sorry," said Danny sympathetically.

"Yeah, well, it's too late for sorry."

"Well, what do you want me to say!" he yelled angrily. "I'm hurting, too. I'm responsible. I haven't had weeks to think about it. Do you realize what a mess we've made? I couldn't concentrate at all today. I played horribly in baseball practice today. Laura, how are we going to tell our parents, friends, relatives? I'm not so sure that we shouldn't get married. If I don't marry you, I'll look like a wimp."

"I don't," said Laura hesitantly. "I can't," she continued with her head facing down. "I don't think we should get married. I'll have the baby, and you can come visit. Next year you can go off to college, and I'll go to a local college here and stay at home."

Laura's voice reflected her frustrations. Danny looked at Laura.

"It's not fair, Laura. It could have happened to so many other kids, but it happened to us."

Danny looked stunned, still trying to cope with the fact that within six months he would be a daddy. Laura gently walked forward and wrapped herself around Danny. They stood silently, embraced in each other's arms.

"Laura, I don't think we need to go to the clinic to seek advice. I know we're both mature individuals."

"Let's go talk to our parents. I'll tell my parents it's best that we don't get married. I know they'll be angry with me; but in the long run, it will be the best thing for you and me if we're going to make this work," said Laura.

They remained embraced in each other's arms.

"Laura, I'm not sure your mom and dad would want it like that. I could find a part-time job, and we could live in an apartment for a while."

"Danny, please," she retorted, "don't say that. Let's live apart for a while. Let's see how it goes. I know you'll be by every-day. I'll drop out of school and take my G.E.D."

Tears ran down Danny's face as he realized the damage that had been done.

"Laura," he said, "I'm so sorry. I can't believe this is happening. I feel as if I'm in a trance."

This time Laura reassured Danny. "I've dealt with this a little longer than you have. This is the only way and the best way for us. I love you, Danny. I know you love me. I'm scared, and I know you are too. I hope that in a few years we can look back at this and say we made the right decision. I know the next painful step we must take now is to tell our parents." Laura took a deep breath.

Danny put his right arm around Laura's neck, and Laura's arm went around his waist as they walked to the car.

"Danny, I think it's best that you tell your parents; and call me when you are through. Hopefully, they'll agree to come with you to tell my parents. I'll prepare them, somewhat, so that Mom won't fall apart so badly."

Laura lay her head on Danny's shoulder as he drove her home.

"I'll see you tonight, Danny," she said as she closed the door and walked around the car. She bent over and gave Danny a kiss on the lips.

"I love you, Laura," he said sweetly.

"Good luck!" she added as she walked into her house.

CHAPTER FOURTEEN

"Hi, sweetheart. Did you have a good time?" Laura brushed her fingers through her hair. "Oh, it was great, Mom."

A sudden frown became apparent on Mrs. Garza's face. "Sweetheart, your eyes look red and swollen. Are you all right?"

Laura gave a tired sigh, "Mom, where's Dad?"

"Why, he's in the dining room finishing up his dinner. Why? Is something wrong?"

Mrs. Garza had a look of fear, almost as if she knew Laura was about to say something horrible. A deep voice came from across the living room, "What's going on?"

Laura gently grabbed her mom's hand and took her into the dining room. Her eyes met with her daddy's.

"Hi, sweetheart."

"Hi, Dad. Mom could you sit down?"

"Laura wants to talk to us, honey," she said as she nervously pulled a chair out and plopped herself in it. Mr. and Mrs. Garza sat looking into Laura's eyes as she began to muster up courage to tell them about her pregnancy.

"I love you, Mom and Dad. I love you both very much. The reason I haven't told you what I am about to tell you is because I didn't want to hurt you. I don't know how to say it, so I'm just going to say it," she said as tears began rolling down her face. "Please, don't get angry at me. I blame no one but myself."

"Go ahead, dear," said Mr. Garza. "Nothing you could tell us could be so bad. Don't feel bad if you didn't get into Harvard," he said mockingly.

Laura's hands covered her face. "Dad, please, don't make this more difficult than it already is. Mom, Dad, I'm...I'm...," Laura took a deep breath. "I'm so embarrassed. I feel really stupid about what I am about to tell you. I'm pregnant."

They sat stunned from what they had just heard.

"I thought about alternatives, but I couldn't go through with them. I've ruined all my chances for college. I know. My life is going to take a turn for the worse. I know it. There's nothing I can do."

Mrs. Garza burst into tears, stood up from her chair, and rushed to her room.

Mr. Garza exploded with anger. He hit the table with his fist. "Where is he? I'd just like to get one punch at him."

Laura was scared. Her father had never looked at her this way. His eyes turned red with anger. He continued to curse Danny. "Wait until I get my hands on him. You didn't do this all by yourself."

Laura sat paralyzed, surprised she wasn't crying heavily.

"How could you?" he yelled at her. He grabbed the

fruit bowl and threw it to the floor. "We trusted you."

"Daddy, please, stop!" she yelled as she covered her ears from the loud sound from the hundreds of pieces of broken glass. Sandra and Peter came running down the hall.

"What is it?" asked her sister and brother as they walked into the dining room.

"Get back in your rooms!" yelled Mr. Garza.

Laura put her hands over her face. She wished this nightmare would be over. Her shame had no limit. "Daddy, please. I didn't intend for this to happen. I wish it would go away."

"What's wrong, Laura?" asked her sister.

Mr. Garza slammed his hands on the table and yelled, "Get out of here! Go to your rooms! NOW!"

"All this time we trusted you, believed you were doing the right thing, and believed you were staying out of trouble!"

Laura could take no more. She pushed her chair back and ran out the kitchen door to the backyard. In a daze, Laura sought shelter behind her favorite cottonwood tree. She was relieved that it was over. On the other hand, she was afraid of what the future would hold as a result of her carelessness.

CHAPTER FIFTEEN

*A*s Danny parked his car in his garage, a sudden shiver ran down his spine. He saw his parents' cars were at home. Uptight and nervous about how badly they would respond to his announcement, Danny walked into the kitchen. "Hi, Mom."

"Hi, sweetie. Is everything back to flowers and roses with you and Laura?" she asked confidently with a grin on her face. She poured the dish liquid into the sink and began washing dishes.

Danny looked nervously at her. "Mom, where's Dad?"

"He's in the bedroom where he always is about this time."

"Danny," she said worriedly, "are you all right? You seem a bit fidgety."

"I'm fine, Mom," he said, trying to reassure her. He stood by the counter and nervously tapped his fingers. "Mom, could you come with me to the living room. I...I need to talk with you and Dad."

"Sure, dear, just let me finish up the...Danny you're sweating. Is something wrong?" she asked.

"Please, Mom."

Mrs. López took the kitchen dish towel and quickly dried her hands. Danny held his hand out to her and silently guided her into the living room. Mrs. López felt a sudden, cold feeling rush through her stomach.

"Oh, my, this is some serious, bad news. I don't like this feeling, Danny. Honey?" she called from the living room.

"Yes, dear," answered Mr. López as he sat in his bedroom with his remote changing channels on the television.

"It's Danny. He needs to talk with us," she replied with a worried look on her face. "I think it didn't go well on his entrance exams."

Danny ran his fingers through his hair. "Mom, could you please stop jumping to conclusions."

"That's okay, dear. He still has another year," remarked Mr. López as he walked into the living room and sat in his favorite chair. "What's up?" he asked.

"Mom, Dad," said Danny as he nervously paced back and forth. "I have something to say that is going to change my entire life. I just found out about it yesterday. I'm not sure how to say it. I'm just going to say it. Before you try to blame someone, I want to tell you that I take full responsibility for my mistakes."

"Go on, son. What are you trying to tell us?" asked his father curiously. He grabbed his wife's hand, feeling that what his son was going to tell him would hurt.

"Mom, Dad. Laura...Laura, my girlfriend, is pregnant."

Silence permeated the room for a long moment. Danny did not continue to talk. He wanted to give them time to absorb the news.

"What?" asked his mom in a whispered voice. "How? Where? I don't understand. You haven't even been with Laura for months. Are you sure it's yours?"

Danny kneeled down on one knee and gently grabbed his mama's hand. "Don't you see? That's why, Mom. Laura was angry at me and at herself and didn't know how to deal with the situation."

"Do her parents know?" she asked as tears slowly rolled down her face. She put her hand to Danny's cheek.

"She's telling them now. Dad, please. I'm as stunned as you are. I'm so sorry. I know I let you down."

Mr. López's eyes turned red as if he wanted to cry. Yet, his manly pride kept him from it. He stood up from the sofa and walked to the window.

"My baby, my dear baby," cried Mrs. López as she hugged Danny.

"Well, son, I guess you just became a man and a father all at once," Mr. López said as he looked Danny in the eyes. "Gosh, and you're only seventeen." He ran his fingers through his hair. "We'll be grandparents at forty. Iris, can you believe it?" he remarked as he turned and looked at her. "Well, son, have you thought about what you are going to do? You just opened up Pandora's box. Welcome to the real world. Have you thought about where you're going to find a job? You realize, no more sports."

Danny did not reply. He continued to look down.

Danny gently put his mama's hands back in her lap

and stood up. "Dad, I don't know what's going to happen. I don't even think Laura truly wants to marry me. I know I'll be a father in less than six months. I have to be a man and follow through on my actions. You taught me that, Dad."

Mr. López turned to Danny, took another deep breath, and put his hands in his pockets. "What are you going to do?"

Danny also took a deep breath. "I think I would appreciate it if both you and Mom would drive with me to Laura's house and help me talk with her parents. I know they're going to be awfully disappointed in their daughter." Tears rolled down Danny's face as he finished.

Mr. López walked over to Mrs. López, took her arm, and embraced her. Loud cries filled the room. "It's okay, dearest. Look at it this way. We'll be gaining a daughter and a baby all at the same time." Mrs. López continued to sob. Mr. López gently stretched his arm to Danny and summoned him to come. The three embraced. His dad gave him a quick, rough pat on his back. "We'll support you in your decision. We love you unconditionally. Whatever your choice, your mother and I will honor it."

Danny felt strong and free as his parents continued to embrace him.

Laura sat in her backyard on the picnic table. The crying had stopped, and a gentle breeze was blowing through her hair. She welcomed it. It gently touched her face and gave her a feeling of peace. She shut her eyes, turned her face up toward the sky, hoping these peaceful minutes would never end.

Suddenly, a soft touch to her shoulder brought her back to reality, "Laura, honey. I think you need a blanket to keep you warm."

Laura welcomed the gesture in silence.

"Oh, and here. I thought you might be hungry," said her mom as she handed Laura a bowl of popcorn.

"Oh, Mom," said Laura as she reached over to hug her. "I've ruined everything. Daddy's dreams, your dreams...."

"Sh, sh, sh," Mrs. Garza gently hugged Laura and gave her a slight pat on her back. "Sh, sh. It's going to be all right. Don't talk anymore. We'll talk about it tomorrow."

"Dad is so angry with me, Mom. He wants to beat up Danny." Mrs. Garza wiped Laura's tears from her face.

"They're just angry emotions he's expressing. He can't believe it. He had such high hopes for you. He feels as if you're still his baby, his oldest and favorite child. He's shattered." Mrs. Garza gave a hopeful smile. "But listen, my dear, it's not as if you've died. It's just a little inconvenience. Soon you'll be back on your feet. You'll finish school and college. We'll manage. What's important right now is that you deliver a healthy baby for us. So crying isn't going to help things. You made your choice, and we'll stand by you."

"That's another thing, Mom. I'm not ready to have a baby now. I'm not even a good sister."

Mrs. Garza sat next to Laura. "Sh...sh. You'll learn, just as you'll have to learn to adjust to other changes in your life."

"Mom, I'm so scared," she continued as tears proceeded to sting her eyes. As they sat embraced in each other's arms, they heard the kitchen door open and close. "Come on, honey, get up. It's late, and we need to go inside. Someone's coming. I believe it's your dad."

"Laura," Mr. Garza said as he approached them. "Danny and his parents are here to talk." Laura looked into her daddy's eyes and could see his soul deeply crushed. Laura ran to her father like a lost child. He hugged her tightly and said, "Oh, my baby. What did you go and do to yourself?"

"I am so sorry, Daddy. I never meant to hurt you. Please find it in your heart to forgive me."

"Understand one thing," he said suddenly as he pushed her away from him and grabbed her face. "You made a mistake, and you will pay for it dearly. But, you don't have to marry him if you don't want to. Think wisely, my child. If you feel marrying him would only make two mistakes, please don't do it. You can stay with us."

Laura looked at him with tears running down her face. The words he said were music to her ears. Deep down inside she already knew that marriage for her and Danny would only be a failure. She also knew Danny was not ready for it. Mr. Garza took Laura's hand in his and put his arm around her while Mrs. Garza quietly followed behind. Mrs. Garza knew there was no point in discussing the situation. Laura had already made up her mind months before, and she would stand firm. Her face frowned sadly. She thought about how Laura's decision would affect every member of their family— Laura in particular.

"Thank you, Daddy. Thank you. Now come on. Let's go inside and talk about the future."

As they walked into the house, Mr. Garza stopped and remarked, "You know, Laura, it wasn't so long ago you were a child yourself. I remember holding you in my arms." His face filled with joy as he continued to tell Laura specific details of her childhood. It was almost as if he went back in time. Laura's spirits were lifted. She felt back on track. She chuckled like a child, happy about life. It was as if for a moment their hearts were at a standstill, and their memories were beautiful.

"Sunshine of my life, I remember you on the swings," Mr. Garza said pointing to the corner where the swings once stood. "You'd swing so high, and the sun's glow would give your hair a golden look. I told you every time you did that you'd get kissed by the sun, and your hair would turn even more golden. So, every day in summer, you'd go out and swing on the swings and ask me if your hair was kissed by the sun. Your cheeks would turn so pink; we were sure you'd found your mommy's make-up box. I'd call you sunshine because that's what you were. And that's what you'll always be to me, no matter what happens." He patted her hands together and gave them a sweet, gentle kiss.

"I love you, Dad."

"I love you, sweetheart."

As they walked into the living room, a sense of tension once again permeated the room. Mr. and Mrs. López and Danny had been welcomed into the house by Laura's sister and brother. Laura could not look them in the eye. She felt embarrassed. As the family finished their greetings and shaking hands, Laura's eyes met Danny's. Almost as if to give her away, Mr. Garza gently directed Laura to go stand next to Danny. Laura conceded.

"Could everyone take a seat?" asked Mr. Garza, in control of the situation. He nervously coughed to clear his throat. "As you know, our daughter Laura is pregnant; and your son Danny is responsible."

Danny nervously interrupted Mr. Garza. "We're both responsible."

"Yes," said Mr. López reluctantly.

"Laura and Danny, have you thought about what you're going to do?"

Laura looked at Danny and took a deep breath, "Well, we don't have many choices. We thought it out up to this point, telling our parents."

"Oh, my dear," interrupted Mrs. López, "you poor child. You knew about this and kept it to yourself all these months. Poor child."

Laura smiled and said, "That's okay, Mrs. López. I'm okay."

Danny put his arm around Laura. She snuggled next to him. Danny nervously ran his fingers through his hair. "Well, school is almost over. I can get a full-time job for the summer and save money before the baby arrives. When school starts, I'll either have to drop out, depending on how things are, or work after school."

"No...No...No... dear," interrupted his mom, "we insist that you stay with us until both of you graduate from school."

"Well, why can't they live here with us?" questioned Mrs. Garza. "Laura is our daughter."

Voices began to rise.

"Well, he is our son; and since he is the man of the household, I think it's our duty that he stay with us until he can spread his wings."

The commotion made Laura want to slip behind the sofa and hide.

"Mom, Dad, please!" said Danny, raising his voice. "Did anyone ask me what we want?"

Laura looked at Danny with a crushed look on her face. How dare he, she thought. First, it's our parents making decisions for us. Now he's making decisions for me.

"I've decided. We're not staying anywhere. Laura and I will work until the baby is born. Then I will continue working."

Laura felt herself becoming angry. Rage filled her.

"How could you?" she asked as she stood up. "Danny, we haven't even discussed this."

"Laura, I know what I'm doing." Danny stood firm.

"No, please, I don't want to get married. I've thought about this for a long time. Danny, you need to finish school.

You need that scholarship. I'm staying with my parents. I don't care what people say. I am not going to marry you, and that's final."

Mr. Garza had a sudden boost of courage. "That's right. If my daughter doesn't want to marry your son, then that's the way it will be."

Mrs. Garza stood with her hands over her mouth, "Dios mio. But... but... they have to get married. That's just the way it should be. Laura, piensaló bien."

Laura ran out of the living room and closed the door to her bedroom. A great feeling of relief ran through her body. What she dreaded most was over.

"Danny, are you all right?" asked Mrs. Garza. She walked over to him and gripped his arm. "I am so sorry this is so stressful. Laura is under so much stress; and, well, a woman's hormones tend to go off a little more than usual when she is pregnant. You understand, don't you, Mr. and Mrs. López?"

The López family prepared to leave. Mr. López stood up and shook Mr. Garza's hand and said, "Yes, Mrs. Garza, it's such a stressful position to be in. We'll talk tomorrow."

Danny walked to Laura's bedroom and softly knocked on her door.

"Laura?"

Laura slowly opened the door.

Danny stood in the doorway, his hands in his pockets.

"Laura, I'm sorry about what happened back there. I

thought you wanted what I wanted."

"I do, Danny. Only not now."

"I love you, Laura; and I'm going to stand by you, no matter what." Laura's eyes smiled as she looked up at Danny. "What an extremely good looking, intelligent guy he is," she thought.

"I love you, Danny."

"I'll see you tomorrow. Get some sleep."

"You too," she said as she reached and kissed him good night.

Danny ran his hand through his hair and said, "I'm so glad this is over."

The morning sun sneaked into Laura's bedroom window. Laura turned over and put the pillow over her face, wanting desperately to go back to sleep. She kicked off the covers. "Oh, my goodness," she whined. "It seems as if I just fell asleep."

As she reached over to turn off her alarm clock, a soft knock came from her door. "Darling, it's Mom. May I come in?" Mrs. Garza walked in with a tray of milk and a bowl of hot oatmeal. A few months ago, Laura would have become disgusted just looking at it. At this stage in her pregnancy, she welcomed the breakfast.

"Good morning. Did you sleep well, sweetheart?"

"Yes, I did Mom." she replied, not wanting to worry her. Laura grabbed the bowl of oatmeal and sat back on her bed.

"Mom, you're not dressed to go to work," she said with half a mouth full of oatmeal.

"Well, dear, I discussed it with your father. I decided to take the day off from work to go with you for a medical checkup to make sure you're okay. We need to get you started on vitamins and find out how far along you truly are."

"Mom, I'm healthy. You don't have to worry."

Mrs. Garza brushed the hair away from Laura's face and said sweetly, "You need to learn what changes your body is going to go through and what to expect."

"Can't we do it over the telephone? I'm really embarrassed about all this."

"I know you are," she continued, gently touching Laura's face. "It will be okay. Come on, get dressed; and we'll begin our day, sweetheart," she said. She picked up the tray and walked out of the room.

"Okay. Let me call Danny and let him know I won't be going to school."

As Danny drove up to the parking lot at San Manuel High, he realized that this time next year his life would not be the same. His life would be changed forever. Trying to come to terms with reality was a lot tougher than what he had envisioned. He felt scared and confused. He loved Laura, but he was also relieved that she did not want to marry.

He walked to the locker in a daze. His appearance reflected his feelings. His uncombed hair and sloppy T-shirt added to his depression. He even wore his thongs instead of his tennis shoes. Danny was oblivious to what he was wearing and also to the fact that no one was around the hall. The tardy bell had already rung. Danny didn't seem to be bothered by it. His mind was occupied with the idea of being a father. The thought simply dumbfounded him. It just couldn't be happening.

He tried to figure out what night it happened, but he couldn't remember. What about sports? How would this affect his performance? Basketball was his number one sport. How could he work and go to practice? That was going to be impossible. Danny wished he could make the problem go away. Yet, every time he tried to dismiss it, reality hit him hard. He couldn't think of anyone he'd known in this dilemma and wondered how he'd make it through.

"Maybe Laura was right not wanting to marry me," he thought. She sure had had more time to think about it. As he looked at his watch, he finally realized he'd already missed half of first period. He decided to drive around in his car. Surely, someone could give him some answers. There had to be a way out of this. Ashamed, scared, and confused, Danny spent the rest of the week going through the denial stage.

Laura plopped herself on the Lazyboy chair and pushed against it with her hands to make it pull out to support her feet. "Mom, I'm so tired. I'm glad it's over. I can't believe they made me go through all those examinations."

"Well, you want a healthy baby, don't you?"

"Yes, I guess," said Laura, tired.

"Well, this is the best way to attain that goal."

Laura could see her mother was not going to stand on the side lines. No, she was going to get as involved as she possibly could.

"Mom, what do you think?"

Mrs. Garza raised her eyebrows. "What do I think about what?" she asked.

Laura kicked her shoes off. "About my decision not to marry Danny."

"Oh. That's a big decision and one you should make on your own."

"I know. But what do you think?"

"I think you're awfully young to be making these decisions. But since you're growing up, decision making is an extremely important part of it. If you truly feel that not marrying Danny is what is best for you and the baby, then we'll support your decision."

Laura yawned. "I'm really tired. I think I'll take a nap." She pushed the Lazyboy chair back into an upright position with her feet and stood up.

"Okay. Dinner will be ready in about two hours."

"Ma," she said with a smirk on her face, "don't make such a fuss over me."

CHAPTER SIXTEEN

*D*anny parked his car in the garage. His stomach began to growl. He looked at his watch as he opened the front door to his house. "Wow, where does the time go? Seven already. I'm missing supper," he thought.

"Hi, Mom!"

She popped her head through the kitchen door. "Hi, sweetheart. How was school today?"

"Okay."

"Laura called you twice. Where have you been?"

"I went over to El Rey restaurant with some of the guys."

"You hungry?"

"Starving. I'll go wash up." As Danny washed his hands, he wondered if he should call Laura and ask how her day went. He wasn't too sure he wanted to know. Suddenly, the phone rang.

"Danny, it's for you."

"I'll get it in my room, Mom." Danny picked up the phone and kicked off his thongs.

"Hello, Danny."

"Hi, Laura. How was your day?"

"Tiring. How was yours?" Laura twisted the telephone

wire around her middle finger.

Danny took a deep breath. "Busy."

"I guess so. Is that why you haven't called me all day? Are you okay?"

"Yeah."

"I know I haven't given you much time to adjust to it."

"Don't worry. I'm okay."

"Hey, I'm about to have supper. I'll call you tonight about 9:00. Okay? Bye," said Danny.

The following morning, Laura woke up with an incredible appetite. She reached across the breakfast table for some toast and orange juice. "Hi, Dad. Good morning, Sandra and Peter."

"Is everything going to be okay?" asked Peter worriedly.

"Sure everything is going to be okay."

"Well, of course, she's going to be all right," insisted her sister in a sassy manner. "It will be a baby girl," she replied as she stood up from the breakfast table.

"No, it won't, dumbbell. It's going to be a boy," Peter retorted aggressively.

Sandra stuck her tongue out. "Girl."

Peter shrugged his shoulders. "Boy."

Her voice began to grow louder. "A girl."

Peter's voice grew angry. "A boy."

"Girl!" yelled Sandra.

"Boy!" yelled Peter.

"Okay, you two!" yelled Mr. Garza "Cut it out. Whatever it is, you'll love the baby."

"I think that's Anna honking for you, dear."

"Bye, Mom. Bye Dad," called Laura.

"Take care, sweetheart."

Laura ran out of the house. For a moment she forgot she was pregnant until her mom reminded her.

"Dear, don't run. You don't want to hurt the baby."

"Mom!" she yelled, embarrassed. "See you later."

"Hi, Anna," Laura said as she hopped into the car.

"Hi, Laura," remarked Anna. She shifted the car from reverse to drive. Anna looked surprised. "You sure look happy. What's up?"

"Nothing."

"I know what's up. But, no, you didn't tell me. I had to find out through the grapevine."

"You know?" Laura blurted in a surprised voice.

"Yes, of course."

Laura's face grew confused. "He wasn't supposed to tell anyone."

"No one told me anything. I saw you!"

"You saw us? What are you talking about?" asked Laura, confused.

"I saw you and Danny get back together. He asked you to go steady and presented you with a promise ring he's been carrying around for a couple of months."

Laura was absolutely lost in thought.

"What?" Is there something else going on?" asked Anna.

"No," blurted Laura. She changed the radio station.

"I mean, oh, my God. Please, don't tell me you didn't know. I let the cat out of the bag, didn't I? Something tells me you don't know anything about a promise ring," said Anna.

"I didn't," Laura confessed. "Settle down."

"Kevin didn't say it was a secret. Danny has had it for quite a while. Shoot. I put my foot in my mouth. Laura, do me a favor and act as if you don't know what's going on. Please, I'll look like the town crier."

"Okay, don't worry. I'll act surprised," Laura said, relieved that Anna and the rest of the school did not know about her pregnancy. She and Danny had agreed that no one would find out until summer. This way she wouldn't have to put up with the students staring at her. But Laura was stunned. Danny was going to give her a promise ring before he knew she was pregnant. Now that he knew of the pregnancy, would he still give her the ring?

"I'm surprised Danny didn't pick you up."

"He was busy," Laura answered, trying to dodge the comment. She knew that Danny was probably in a daze as she had been when she first learned of her pregnancy. "Anna, what about you and Kevin? I've heard lots of rumors."

"Oh, really? Like what?" she asked smiling.

"Well, one rumor is that you two are going steady and are really hot. Is that true?" As they approached a stop sign, Anna reached to change the radio station.

"Yeah, you could say that. What else have you heard?"

"Let's cut to the chase. You tell me; then I'll get it straight from the horse's mouth."

Anna smiled proudly, "The truth is, I really like him a lot; and I know he likes me too. We've gone out several times. My mom really likes him. I don't think it will be too hard to persuade Dad to let me go out with him." As they drove into the parking lot of San Manuel High, they saw Kevin. Anna looked at Laura.

"Well, go on, silly. He's waiting for you," said Laura with a grin on her face.

"I'll see you later," whispered Anna as she stepped out of the car.

Kevin walked to the car and said, "Hi Laura."

"Hi, Kevin," she answered.

"Hi, Anna," said Kevin as he gave her a light kiss on the lips. He took Anna's hand, and they walked dreamily to the classrooms. Kevin put his hand in his pocket. "Anna, do you want to go to see a movie tonight?"

"Sure," said Anna comfortably. "What are they showing?"

"Blackprint."

"Blackprint. Sounds good." Anna had never heard of the movie but didn't really care. As long as she was with Kevin, nothing really mattered.

As Laura walked to the locker, her heart began to beat faster. She realized Danny was nowhere to be found. A quick, sharp shiver ran through her body as she hustled to get her books, so she'd have enough time to walk past Danny's class. She walked quickly, trying to regain her composure. Feelings of anger and shame ran through her. "Stupid girl," she thought. She peeked into Danny's class, and she saw familiar faces.

"Hi, Laura," said Bianca.

"Hey, Danny, it's Laura," said another male voice. Laura was oblivious to the students. Danny looked withdrawn. He stood up and walked out of the class.

Laura tried to keep from screaming at him. She maintained a dignified presence. "I waited for you by the lockers. Where were you?"

Danny leaned back on the door avoiding eye contact. "I had to do some work. Look, why don't you get off my back?"

"Why didn't you call me last night or pick me up this morning?" Laura put her hand on his shoulder.

"What is this? One hundred questions? I was tired last night and busy this morning."

Laura felt betrayed. She had never imagined Danny's reaction to be like this. She decided to head for class before tears began to race down her face.

Laura tried to bury herself in her classes. Her lunch was

simply milk and Doritos and then back to class. She was relieved when the last bell of the day rang. Now all she had to do was head to debate practice. She and Thelma had neglected it these past few months.

The school had an intellectual reputation for excellence in debate. The teacher would have them practice off season so that they would be ready the following year and once again win the state finals. "Thelma is a terrific partner," Laura thought. "She is dedicated and sharp." Winning the last three state finals had a lot to do with Thelma's performance.

It was late April and Laura was curious as to why Thelma was here so late in the month. Since her parents were migrant workers, the family usually left in early April. Laura took a deep, relaxing breath before she entered Mrs. Medrano's class.

"Hello, Mrs. Medrano."

"Hello, Laura."

"Where's Thelma?"

Mrs. Medrano stared at Laura as if she'd lost something. "Thelma's gone."

"What? What are you talking about?"

"Last week she let me know she would not be in journalism anymore."

"Did she already leave to go up north?"

Mrs. Medrano walked to her desk and began putting papers in order.

"Laura, I'm sorry. I thought you knew. She said she

would talk to you about it. It's worse than that."

Laura prepared herself for more bad news. "What are you saying?" Laura's face filled with worry as Mrs. Medrano put the papers down.

"You see, Laura, Thelma's father had a heart attack. And since Thelma is the oldest, the right thing to do with a family as large as Thelma's is to drop out of school and help make ends meet at home."

"What?" Laura felt as if the floor had moved out from under her. "We just talked a few weeks ago."

"Laura, I'm sorry. Please sit down. It looks as if you're going to faint. You're very pale. I know you and Thelma are good friends. I tried everything." She put her arm around Laura's shoulder, "I'm sorry."

"Good friends," she thought. Thelma was her right hand. These last few months Laura had neglected their friendship. Laura thought that next to Anna, Thelma was the only true friend she had. They weren't constantly together, but that was only because Thelma was from the other side of the tracks. She was poor and had no telephone and had an extremely strict dad. School was the only place they were together. Today was going to be the day that she told only one friend about her depressing life. And now that friend seemed to be in a rotten position herself.

"Laura, are you all right? Here, let me get you a glass of water. Rachel, get a glass of water."

"Mrs. Medrano, here it is!" yelled Rachel as she rushed in from the hall holding the glass of water.

"I'm okay," Laura insisted. She wiped her tears with the edge of her sleeves.

"I had no idea you would react this way."

Laura was upset about Thelma, but she was also still hurt from the quarrel she had with Danny earlier in the day. She felt as if her world was crumbling all around her.

"You know, Laura," said Mrs. Medrano. "I've not given up on Thelma. I'm going to visit her family and ask her father to please reconsider his decision. I'm going to plead with him. But if Thelma drops out of school now to help the family out, it will help for the time being. If she stays in school, the result will be best for her and the family. Thelma is too bright a student to drop out of school and wait on tables. I haven't given up the fight yet," she said. She grabbed Laura's hand and held it firmly. "I'm going to talk to him about statistics and beg him not to let Thelma become one."

Laura felt somewhat relieved. "I'd love to join you, Mrs. Medrano."

"I'd love it. In fact, you would be a great asset."

"Thanks for the glass of water, Rachel."

"No problem. See ya. Good-bye, Mrs. Medrano," called Rachel.

Mrs. Medrano looked down at her watch. "Laura, what are you doing right now?"

"I'm going home. Why?"

"I thought maybe we could go visit Thelma's parents."

"Right now, today?" replied Laura.

"Yes. I mean, I know it's short notice. You see, I'll be at meetings all this week. The only time I have is now."

"Yeah. Sure, Mrs. Medrano. I'll go with you now. Let me go to my locker to get a few things. Great. I'll meet you back here."

"I'll be waiting." Mrs. Medrano walked about the class busily putting things in order for the next day.

Laura hurried to her locker. She thought this would be nice. It would take her mind from her problems. She could concentrate on Thelma's.

Laura stepped in and closed the front door to Mrs. Medrano's car. Mrs. Medrano reminded Laura to fasten her seat belt. Laura felt somewhat uncomfortable. She was sure Mrs. Medrano would notice her stomach now, as it was beginning to protrude.

"Which way do I go, Laura?"

"Turn right to the south side of town."

Mrs. Medrano's face formed a wrinkle between her eyebrows. "Laura, don't you live on the north side of town?"

"Yes, I do," Laura instantly knew what she was getting at. Without Mrs. Medrano asking the next question Laura began, "Thelma and I have been friends since elementary school. We're not cousins. Thelma, Anna, and I became blood sisters when we were young. A pilot project was started by the district. Someone must have complained that the poor students in the lower social-economic barrios or neighborhoods weren't getting equal representation."

Laura continued, "The children from the southside of town who accelerated and scored high on nationwide tests were bused to De La Rosa School." Laura threw her head back and stretched her legs. "That's where I met Thelma. We became instant friends. I almost forgot," Laura crossed her arms. "Anna wasn't enrolled in our classroom, but she went to our school."

"How sweet. No wonder you were so devastated when you heard about Thelma dropping out of school," said Mrs. Medrano.

Laura smiled as she continued, "I remember when we were little girls. During recess, Thelma and I were teachers and Anna was always the student. Finally, we came to an agreement. I would teach her English and science classes, and Thelma would have her for math and history classes. Pretty good compromise."

Laura's face grew dim as another thought entered her mind. "You know, Mrs. Medrano, one Christmas past, when we returned to school from the holiday vacation, our teacher asked us to bring our presents in. During lunch, Thelma was running frantically around the playground. I ran up to her," Laura reminisced. "I asked her, 'What are you doing, Thelma?' She had a folded paper with tape on the ends. She was picking up fire ants and putting them in the bag."

"I need ants. I didn't receive any gifts for Christmas. Santa Claus forgot us and skipped over our house. But I have red ants."

"I peeped into the paper bag and noticed the ants crawling out of the bag. 'Thelma, they'll bite you.'"

"No, they won't, silly," she replied with a sweet smile. "I'll take them home. You take them out by grabbing them by the tail end of their bodies. After that, you put them in water. When they get tired of swimming, you can pretend they are dolls asleep in a matchbox bed. When they awaken, put them in water again. I play with them like dolls until I'm tired of playing."

"I was amazed by Thelma's imagination." Laura remembered Thelma's smiling eyes. "She never felt sorry for the opportunities and material things she didn't have."

"That evening I told my mom what happened—that we were asked to bring our best Christmas toys to class and how Thelma's toy dolls were red ants." Mrs. Medrano listened carefully. "My mom had a sad look on her face and left me in the kitchen. She quickly dressed and dashed out the door. When I asked where she was going, she replied, 'shopping.' That's all I knew. The next morning, Thelma came to school with a brown, curly-haired doll. She said Santa had made two trips. He forgot her on Christmas, so he'd made a special trip for her and her brothers and sisters. What a happy day that was for Thelma. She told the magical story to everyone in class. Her doll could not walk or talk like the others, but her doll did cry. She made it seem as if she had the best doll in the whole world. By the end of class, all the girls, including myself, wanted her doll and had abandoned ours."

Mrs. Medrano smiled. "That's such a sweet ending to a sweet story. Did you ever find out who it was that gave her the doll?" asked Mrs. Medrano.

"Yes, of course. It was my mom. From that Christmas on there were no more mud-made dolls or red ant dolls for Thelma and her siblings."

"Did Thelma ever spend the night at your house?"

Laura put her hand to her chin. "Hmmm, come to think of it, yes, she did, a few times. One was the time my dad and I taught Thelma how to ride a bike. She was about ten. It wasn't that she couldn't learn. It was just that she never had a bike. That year I gave my bike to her, and I received a new one. Her parents let her spend the night. I don't remember all the other times, but one was when we were in junior high before they left to go up north. Yeah," Laura said. "Thelma begged them, and they agreed."

"Hmmm," said Mrs. Medrano. "You just gave me an idea."

Laura looked puzzled, "I did?"

Mrs. Medrano entered the driveway to Thelma's home and turned the car engine off. "Laura, I'm going in. Try to keep the kids outside, so I can try to talk with her parents."

"Of course," Laura said with a nod.

As Mrs. Medrano walked up the steps and into Thelma's house, she concentrated on how she'd carefully try to convince Thelma's parents that she should stay in school...without offending them. Laura waited a few minutes before she stepped out of the car.

Mrs. Medrano walked up ahead. The line of children seemed to come from everywhere. The two youngest children stepped out of the house and came running as if they hardly ever had company. Mrs. Medrano was greeted and invited in. Three other brothers and sisters came from behind the house. Along the side, two mangy, happy dogs were wagging their tails and barking, which put Laura on alert.

Laura smiled as she saw the resemblance among the children and Thelma. Laura jumped over the pot holes in the driveway. Heads peaked through the screen windows, and faces soon revealed themselves.

Laura tried not to notice the neighborhood's small homes. Most of them were made of wood with aluminum nailed to the top. Many window frames did not have windows, only screens. Some homes were so small the people sat outside watching the cars storm by, most leaving a thick mask of smelly dust. As Laura stood there, she remembered the orange groves where Thelma sought refuge as a young girl. They were now poor residential homes. This was worse than the ghettos. Dogs were running around, some with hardly any fur on their skin. Laura composed herself. She recognized Thelma's sister Myra and approached her.

"Hi, Myra," she smiled and leaned forward to embrace her. "How've you been?"

Myra blushed as Laura's eyes dilated from how much Myra's stomach protruded.

"Myra! How? When? No wonder I haven't seen you at school." She stood with her hands crossed over her stomach.

"Didn't Thelma tell you?" She waved her hand in the air. "Oh, of course. She is kind of embarrassed about the situation."

Laura tried to ignore the tension that was beginning to hang invisibly around them. "You look beautiful, Myra."

Myra looked surprised. For once, negative criticism did not start a conversation.

Laura put her arm around Myra's shoulder. "You'll make a good mamma even if you are only fifteen years old."

Myra wiped the sweat from her forehead and put her hand over her soft, green eyes to keep out the evening sun. "Mom and Dad said I could attend the program where pregnant girls go after they've had their babies. I'll learn to be a good mother and continue classes," she said, rather drearily.

"You'll be fine." The conversation seemed to be going nowhere. Laura wasn't sure how she could change the subject.

Suddenly, from across the street, came a young boy in his early teens. He had a red bandana tied around his head. His pants dropped below the waist. He had on black, shiny shoes. Who was he? "Could it be?" questioned Laura silently.

Myra shrugged her shoulders. "Oh great. Here comes my goofy brother."

"Hey, Laura. Don't you remember me?"

Laura was surprised. "Beto, is that you?"

"Yeah, man. What's up?"

Laura smiled. "The last time I saw you, you were a little boy in elementary school. You were in the accelerated third-grade class. Thelma and I were in sixth grade." She stood thinking, "Yeah, yeah, we were —"

"Yeah," he said not wanting to talk about it. He moved to take a chuco pose before continuing. "That's not cool around here. I'm back with the crew."

"The what, Beto?" asked Laura.

He flipped out his hands and made a sign. "That's my gang, 'Chicanos with an attitude.'" He pointed across the street.

Laura saw kids no older than fourteen years old lighting up cigarettes. They all wore the same color bandanas over their foreheads and black pants that didn't seem to fit.

Myra's eyes rolled back. She concentrated on untangling her curly, black hair. "Yeah, that gang is so stupid," she remarked.

"Shut up, Myra. It's not my fault one of the boys knocked you up."

"You're such a jerk." Myra took a defensive stand.

"Yeah, well. You're a loser, too, jerk."

Laura quickly tried to lessen the tension of the situation by telling a joke. The joke seemed to do the trick.

"Yeah. I'll be an uncle at sixteen. Pretty cool," Beto said in a hoarse voice. Smiles were exchanged between brother and sister.

"Well, so, what grade are you in?" asked Laura.

"In school? I dropped out. That's not for me," continued Beto, portraying a tough, macho image.

Laura smiled nervelessly. "Well, then, how did you keep up with your stylish dress?"

A smile and sudden silence passed through the air. Non-verbal communication took place. Beto put his hands in his pockets. "Let's just say, I manage."

Laura leaned one side of her hip on the car. The children ran after the dogs. No one seemed to care.

"Hey, Beto!" yelled a voice from across the street. "Your turn, vato."

Beto screamed, "I'm coming, loco!" He flashed a hand sign to Laura. "Hay nos vemos, amiga."

Laura waved good-bye to him, "You take care, Beto." She was disheartened to see one of Thelma's brothers go astray.

Mrs. Medrano sat on a couch inside Thelma's house. Her face grew serious as the conversation about Thelma's good behavior came to an end.

"Les tengo que decir que es la razón que vinimos Laura y yo a hablar con usted señor Muñoz y señora Muñoz. No queremos que se salga Thelma de la escuela." She continued her conversation in Spanish, talking about the reasons it was crucial that Thelma graduate from school. She would set an example for her brothers and sisters. Thelma would also have a chance to get out of poverty.

Mrs. Medrano could not guarantee Thelma would graduate in the top five in her senior class or even first in her class next year. She did promise, however, that if Thelma stayed in school, she would receive scholarships to many prestigious universities.

Mr. Muñoz's face lit up with joy. His eyes seemed almost teary. He coughed and sat up to compose himself. "¿Mi Thelma tiene oportunidad de graduar numero uno en su clase, señora Medrano? Ella nunca nos habló de eso. Sabemos que va muy bien en la escuela, pero no tan bien así."

Ms. Muñoz put her hands to her mouth and was amazed. Her eyes, too, became teary. Thelma's siblings ran in and out of the house, slamming the door behind them. Thelma's parents stood in a deep trance, thinking of the possibilities. Mrs. Medrano knew that she did not have to talk anymore. She put her glass of water on the table, shook hands once again, and politely walked out the door.

The screen door made a loud screeching sound as Mrs. Medrano stepped outside on the porch. Mrs. Muñoz walked closely behind her.

Laura approached Mrs. Muñoz. "Hello, Mrs. Muñoz," she said as she embraced her.

Mrs. Muñoz gently touched Laura's face with the back of her hand.

"¡Hola hijita! ¿Cómo estas, linda?"

"Muy bien, gracias."

"Le mandas saludos a tu mamá."

"Si, como no. Con mucho gusto."

Laura and Mrs. Medrano stepped into the car after the handshakes and good-byes. Even as they drove off, Thelma's younger sisters ran after the car—in spite of the dust.

Mrs. Medrano drove slowly, careful not to drive over the pot holes. She had a confident smile as she drove out of the barrio and entered the highway.

"Laura, I think that you and I have made a difference in this world. I think by coming here and talking to Thelma's parents, we may have helped the first of the Muñoz family to graduate and hopefully work her way out of poverty. Most importantly, her younger siblings just may follow in her footsteps."

Laura's face lit up. "Really? What did you say?"

Mrs. Medrano hesitated, being careful not to tell Laura that she and Thelma were nose-to-nose for the top honors in the graduating class next year. "I just told them the truth. I also told them about you and Thelma, about how you two grew up together. I think that's when I hit a cord. That's when Mr. Muñoz finally began to listen."

"There's something about you, Thelma, and Anna. When I was talking about you and Thelma, Mr. Muñoz was looking out the screen door. He noticed you talking to Myra and Beto. I heard him mumble, 'No. My Thelma will make it out of this place.' Mr. Muñoz's face was somber. That's when the magic words appeared."

Laura was absorbed in her conversation. "What magic words?" Her eyes dilated with interest.

"'¡Mi Thelma sí va graduar!' were his last words to me. I'm sure he'll keep his promise."

Laura waved good-bye to Mrs. Medrano as she drove off. Inside she could hear the telephone ringing from the porch.

"Laura," yelled Sandra. "Telephone for you. It's Anna."

"Hello."

"Hi there. Laura, I just wanted to remind you about cheerleading tryouts tomorrow evening."

Laura looked blank, "Oh, my goodness. I had forgotten all about that. I've been so busy."

"How could you forget? Your best friend is trying out. I told you about it last week."

"It just slipped my mind. Sorry."

"Listen, I'll meet you in journalism class. We'll go together."

"Okay. See ya tomorrow. Bye." Laura hung up the telephone. She felt hungry as Danny crept into her memory. She was aware that Danny was avoiding her, yet she decided to do nothing about it. Every time she thought about how Danny was avoiding her, she felt like crying. She'd done great at avoiding her parents questions and not having to talk about her decisions about the baby and her.

"Fine," she thought. "If he is going to avoid me, there is no point in pursuing him." She already felt as if she'd made a spectacle of herself yesterday.

The weekend had arrived and Laura welcomed it with sheer exhaustion. She'd managed to dodge her parents questions about Danny and her. Finals were coming up. She'd simply drown herself in her studies and exit her junior year with superior marks. She plunged into bed and snuggled her pillow. She gave a long, lazy yawn; and she said softly, "I'll just nap for awhile. If I could just forget about my problems for a while and simply rest, just rest." She dozed through the evening.

CHAPTER SEVENTEEN

"*D*anny, here's your hamburger and fries, dude," said Julio as he handed Danny the fries and passed the Coke.

"Don't spill anything in my car, man!" said Danny jokingly.

"Be cool, dude."

They sat quietly and watched the cars going around the drive-in at Stars.

"Hey, Danny, isn't that Nancy? She's not with Rene. It looks like Eddie Galván."

Danny was in no mood to joke. "Julio, could I trust you with something?"

Julio looked puzzled, "Sure, dude. Just don't tell me your like a fag or something."

Danny smirked. "Hey, dude. I'm serious."

Julio looked at Danny and saw concern in his eyes. "Shoot, man."

"I just have to tell someone, get it off my chest."

"Yeah, what is it?" Julio's eyes did not blink. "Laura give you the dump? I'm listening."

Danny smirked, "I wish it was that simple." Danny paused. "Laura ... Laura's pregnant."

Julio looked stunned.

"Are you sure, guy?" Julio's soft, black curls fell to his forehead.

Danny tossed his head back and stretched out as best he could.

"Well...well...have you...you told anyone?"

Danny's palms began to sweat. "Her parents and my parents know."

Julio looked deeply concerned. "Have you thought about what your options are?"

Danny looked frustrated and confused as he continued to have nervous reactions. He popped his fingers, crossed his arms, and put his hand to his mouth. "I'm not sure," he said in a muffled voice. "I guess the right thing to do is marry her."

Julio looked down and away from Danny not knowing what to say. He thought he'd say, "I'm sorry," but wasn't sure that it was the appropriate phrase under the circumstances. "Well," replied Julio nervously, "Is there anything I can do, man?"

Danny flashed a smile, and a handshake was exchanged. "No, it's my problem, my mistake."

Laura hurriedly dressed as she looked at her clock and realized she'd overslept. "Oh, my goodness," she groaned as she looked at the bags under her eyes. "I have to hurry." She quickly brushed her hair and put on mascara and lipstick. It was all she had time for. She dashed out of her bedroom and into the kitchen for breakfast. She followed the enticing smell of chorizo. Everyone had left. A plate on the counter by the stove with chorizo and eggs and hot tortillas quickly caught her attention.

"Hi, honey. I left breakfast for you. Make sure to eat it all and don't forget your prenatal vitamins and milk.

Love,

Mom"

Laura practically swallowed her breakfast whole and drank her milk. She ran to the living room and saw Anna pulling up. Where did the weekend go? She felt as if she had slept all weekend.

"Hi, Anna. Good morning," she said as she opened the car door and sat down.

"Hi, Laura," she said enthusiastically.

Laura immediately noticed something wrong. She noticed Anna wasn't bopping or singing or dancing to the music on the radio. "What's up, Anna?"

Anna bit her fingernails. "Today they tell us if we made the cheerleading squad."

"Is that what you are nervous about?" replied Laura reassuringly. "You know you're on the squad."

"No, I don't. What if people just didn't vote for me because they were sure I'd win anyway." Anna nervously played with her hair.

"Anna, you're not making sense. Don't worry about it."

Anna thumped her hand on the steering wheel. "Did you see me at tryouts?"

"Did I watch you try out? Don't you remember? I took pictures of you, silly. Anna, will you calm down?"

Anna tried to calm down; but as she drove into the school parking lot, she could feel that nauseous feeling in her stomach become worse. "I feel as if I need to throw up. It's my nerves," she said. She quickly parked her car and opened the door.

Laura knew her best friend needed some emotional support. She quickly exited the car, walked over to Anna's side, and grabbed her hand softly. "Anna, you've never had a problem cheerleading. I don't even want to hear this hogwash. Take a deep breath. Now exhale." Anna did as she was told as if she were a child desperately needing direction.

"Feel better?" asked Laura with a smile on her face.

"Yeah."

"Come on. Let's go."

Laura and Anna exchanged farewells and left in different directions for their classes. As the announcements for the day came over the intercom, Anna sat waiting nervously. She thought she'd jump out of her chair. She tried to hide her nervousness by saying good morning to all her classmates. She opened her notebook and shuffled papers as if to put them in order. Suddenly, over the intercom, Principal González announced, "Now, what everyone's been waiting for! The newly elected varsity cheerleaders for next year will be, in alphabetical order...."

Anna tried desperately to smile, as all eyes were on her. "There are only two more positions left and six girls to fill them," she thought.

"Anna Guzmán," said the voice over the intercom. Anna was oblivious to all other names but hers. She jumped from her chair and hugged Jerry out of sheer happiness. Anna smiled and thanked everyone. The class applauded and congratulated her. She breathed a sigh of relief. It was over. Now Anna could shine in her final year of high school. Her plans had gone as she anticipated they would. The rest of the week would be nothing but praise and congratulations for her and the rest of the girls elected to the varsity cheerleading squad.

Laura smiled as she heard Anna's name. She thought, "How wonderful for Anna." Her senior year would be one of fun, glory, and excitement.

As her friends were leaving for college, she would be desperately making applications at the local supermarket. If she were lucky, she might be able to attend night school. Laura looked down in shame. Tears rolled down her face. Students were beginning to notice her tears. Laura walked out of the room. "How could this be happening?" she thought. "Why am I still crying? You'd think I would have become used to it." Laura entered the girls' bathroom intending to go straight into a stall, hoping no one would see her. As she walked in, Anna was walking out. Laura looked stunned.

"Did you hear? I made the cheerleading squad!" yelled Anna with victory in her voice.

"I know that, silly. Congratulations," said Laura as she hugged Anna and tried to hide her tears.

"Hey, but look at you. Laura, you're in tears."

Suddenly, Laura couldn't stand it any longer.

"What's wrong? What are you doing here? Why the tears?"

"Oh, it's nothing. Just hay fever."

"Laura, please. I've known you for too long. You don't get sick, remember, Miss Healthy."

Laura gasped briefly and gave Anna a look of surrender. "Oh, Anna."

"What is it? Laura, next year will possibly be the best year of our lives. Don't forget college. We're going to have a ball, remember? We'll be roommates, and you'll ride off your senior year to college with the best scholarship there is."

"That's just it," said Laura as her voice cracked.

"What? Please tell me?" pleaded Anna. She grabbed Laura by the shoulders.

"None of that's going to happen!" yelled Laura out-of-control. "I won't go to college, or the prom, or even be here next year! You see, Anna, I'm pregnant!"

Anna looked as if a ghost came before her.

"I'm sorry. I don't mean to rain on your party. Didn't you see these over-sized T-shirts I've been wearing? My weight gain?"

Anna stood stunned, "Yes, but a lot of girls wear over-sized shirts." Anna began to wipe the tears from her eyes, "What are you going to do?"

"What can I do, Anna?" she asked. She wiped the tears from her face. "It's over. That's all. Everything I planned for and tried so hard for has disappeared before my very eyes. Now I feel as if I need to re-route my entire life, and I'm not so sure I know how."

Anna hugged Laura. For a while they stood embraced in each other's arms.

"Oh, Anna. I'm so sorry. This is the best day of your life."

"Laura, don't be silly. It's only cheerleading." For a while, they both stood still not knowing what to do or say. Anna gently wiped the tears from Laura's face. "Oh, Laura...oh, Laura. What have you gone and done?" she asked as she gave her best friend another strong, supportive hug.

Laura reacted with relief again. No secrets were kept from the other.

"Well, aren't you going to disown me as your friend? I wouldn't blame you. I feel I've sunk so low. I've hurt my parents, my family, and most of all, myself. And for what? You should have seen the look on my parents' faces when I told them. They tried to be strong, but I know they were truly crushed."

Anna took a Kleenex from her purse and gave it to Laura. "I'm so sorry to hear that. Laura, calm down. I'll never stop being your friend. Don't you know that? And besides, this is only temporary. You'll have your baby...in what?" she thought as she counted the months.

"November," blurted Laura. "It's not that simple, Anna. My life will never be the same again. What can I do, Anna?" she said hoping desperately to hear the right answers. Her voice was distorted by her crying. "It's all over. That's all. It took me seven years to decide and to prepare for what I wanted to do after I graduated from high school." She took a long breath, "Yet, in one moment of passion, my world came crumbling down. My life changed in every way possible."

"Laura, why did you keep this to yourself?

Anna suddenly remembered all the times Laura turned her down on weekends or refused to go to parties. "This was the reason. You poor thing. Oh, Laura."

"Do you know the worst thing about this whole matter, Anna? I'm so embarrassed for my parents. I'm so scared of what people are going to think of me. This kind of thing is supposed to happen to bad girls. You know," she continued tossing her hair over her shoulders, "the girls who sleep around with all sorts of guys."

"Sh, sh, sh. Oh, Laura, you're not a bad girl. And if I hear anyone saying so, I'll punch them right in the face." Anna clasped Laura's hand to her. "Besides, this proves that it can happen to the prettiest, smartest, sweetest girl in school."

Laura looked at Anna and smiled.

"Come on," she said with a smile on her face. "Now, it's all coming back to me." Dumbfounded, Anna hit her forehead with the palm of her hand. "That's why you were so hungry."

Laura giggled between tears.

"Come on. I'll drive you home."

Laura caught Anna by the arm, "What am I doing? This is practically the happiest time of your life, and here I am taking it away from you."

"Don't be ridiculous, silly."

Anna again turned to Laura and clasped her hand between her hands. "Listen. I don't know what is going to happen, but I know everything is going to be fine. I know it," she replied with a smile.

"Oh, Anna. I'm so glad to have you as my best friend."

"Tell me. I want to hear all about it. Does Danny know?"

"Yes," said Laura annoyed, "and so do his parents. But he is being a real jerk. I really don't care," she said with hurt.

"Are you guys going to get married?"

Laura looked shocked at Anna and remarked almost insultingly. "Are you kidding? I've made one mistake. Why make two?"

"Laura, you two love each other. How do you figure it's a mistake?"

"That's exactly why. We love each other. I've been reading a lot on teen pregnancy, enough to know that statistics are extremely high on divorce among teenage marriages."

"Yes, Laura, but you and Danny are different."

"Yes, that's correct, Anna. That's why I have to make this sacrifice in order for Danny and me to survive this storm. You see, if I give Danny a chance to educate himself and I educate myself with the help of our parents, we may have a chance for the future." She paused for a minute. "Besides, Anna, in my heart I've no desire for marriage. I know that Danny doesn't either. If we get married only to please everyone who will talk about us, we will only hurt ourselves."

Anna was stunned by the confidence in Laura's speech

and the sincerity in her voice.

"Now, it's your turn to take a deep breath and exhale."

This time, Laura followed obediently. "Anna, you mustn't tell anyone."

"You have my word."

Laura glanced at Anna with disbelief. Anna grasped her hand, "You truly have my word. I won't tell a soul." Anna grinned, "Hmmm...I must admit, you sure did do your homework. Why am I not surprised? You researched teen pregnancy issues quite well and made the best decision for yourself." She gave Laura a strong embrace which reassured Laura that her secret would stay safe between them, at least until her stomach would begin to show signs of life.

"Anna, I'm so exhausted about this issue. I think about it twenty-four hours a day," Laura's eyes locked into Anna's. "Oh, my goodness. Where has the time gone?"

As the girls left the bathroom, Anna, still overwhelmed from Laura's news, was greeted with smiles and congratulations. Suddenly, she was surrounded by friends who shook her hand. Laura quietly disappeared to the back of the crowd and walked away.

As the crowd slowly began to leave, Anna felt the whisk of arms around her waist. "Congratulations, my girl." Anna could not help but smile. "You have the prettiest smile."

"Kevin, you're just saying that."

"Walk you to class?"

"Sure."

"Congratulations, Anna," called different friends from across the hall.

"Thanks."

"You deserve it, Anna. Hey, what do you say we go out and celebrate tonight with all our friends?" asked Kevin.

"That sounds great!"

Anna was overwhelmed with joy, especially as rumors spread that she would probably be the head varsity cheerleader. As the last class came to an end, Anna could hardly wait to get to cheerleading practice. She knew it was time to elect the new head cheerleader.

"Okay, girls," said Mrs. Carter. "Congratulations. I guess it's okay to take a break for today. All of you deserve a pat on the back. Each and every one of you deserve and earned it. Now it's time to elect a head cheerleader."

Anna's heart began to beat swiftly. There were ten varsity cheerleaders: four juniors, two sophomores, and four seniors, all who hoped to be head cheerleader. As Mrs. Carter passed the pieces of paper on which each cheerleader would cast her vote, tension was apparent. You could hear the popping of fingers and popping of necks. Nervous coughs circled the air.

Mrs. Carter collected the folded pieces of paper and started to count. Minutes seemed like hours, and it seemed the counting would never end.

"It's official," she said with a smile. "I'm sure she will make a fine head cheerleader and so will the head captain. The co-head captain for next year is Shelly Fung." The room was filled with the sound of clapping. "Our new head cheerleader is Anna Guzmán."

"Yeah!" yelled the girls. Once again, hugs and wishes were given. The four graduating seniors were present.

"Well, Anna, what's your first order of business?" asked Shelly.

Anna was speechless. Tears rolled down her face.

"Come on. Don't cry," said Shelly.

She slowly stood up from the Indian-sitting position. She looked at the circle of girls. "I'd like to say something to the departing seniors: Michelle, Frances, Darcy, and Lolita. You were great. We went to state this year and won. We will never forget. Let's have a round of applause for our senior cheerleaders." As the applause quieted, she continued. "And our incoming cheerleaders, congratulations, as well. Thank you all who elected me head cheerleader. I won't let you down. My first order will be, the rest of practice is off. Let's go celebrate at El Rey restaurant. No dieting tonight."

"All right!" yelled the girls as they stood up and walked out of the gym.

CHAPTER EIGHTEEN

*L*aura walked up the steps to her house. As she entered the living room, she was greeted by Peter and Sandra. Her mom popped her head out of the kitchen. "I'm cooking your favorite food, angel: chicken enchiladas." She thought as she walked to her bedroom, "That's definitely not the right name." She was more like an idiot, a moron. That's what they should be calling her. She began to feel sorry for herself. She plopped herself down on her bed and thought of when she divulged her secret to Anna.

A soft knock came from her bedroom door. "Honey, may I come in? Oh, baby, what's wrong?" asked Mrs. Garza.

"Oh, Mom."

Laura quickly embraced her mom. "Mother, I just don't know if I'm making the right choice or if this is the wrong choice."

Her mother gently stroked Laura's hair and let her finish talking. "Laura, there is no right or wrong choice. The choice you make is the one you can live with in your heart. Once you've thought about the choices and consequences and are willing to take them no matter what, then for you, you've made your choice. That's the right choice."

Laura was comforted by knowing that no matter what happened, it would somehow turn out okay; and her parents would love her unconditionally.

"Laura."

"Yes, Mom?"

The stern frown on her mom's face told Laura that the inevitable question was about to be asked.

"Have you and Danny spoken lately?"

Laura felt the muscles in her neck becoming tense. "Mom, there's nothing to talk about. Danny's being a jerk and pretending it never happened. Laura paced back and forth. I'm going to raise the baby by myself. Mom, I've thought about it. After I have the baby, I'll take courses for a GED. And I'll go to work at the same time. I know there is no way I'll be able to go to Atlantic University. I'll go to the local university, and I'll get my degree. Meanwhile, I won't bother you or Dad. I'll simply rent an apartment. You'll see. It will be all right."

She gently took Laura's hand in hers and paused for a moment. "Laura, it is very important that you realize that you are not alone in this. We are your family, and we love you. Danny will come around in time; and remember, it's not all your problem. Please, sweetheart, please think this through a little more carefully. It will be impossible to do all that and to support yourself and your baby on a minimum wage. Talk to Danny. Don't be so angry. Put your problems aside, and see if you and he can work them out."

"But, Mom..."

"Shh," she said as she put her hand over Laura's mouth. "Remember, most importantly, you have 100 percent of our support; and we love you so much. Granted, we didn't expect a grandchild so soon. But, the baby will be here soon; and we will welcome it with open arms.

Laura smiled. "I love you and Dad so much. Thank God for parents like you. I don't know what I'd do without you," she said as she threw her arms around her mom.

"If you and Danny get married, you can live with us."

Laura pushed back. "Mom, you're not listening. Don't you see? I've read the literature. Did you know, Mom, that for every 100 teenage marriages, 90 end in divorce? Mom," she continued, "I don't want to be another statistic. You see, I'm not sure that Danny's the right guy for me. I know it sounds stupid, but the thought of marriage never entered my mind. I'm not going to marry Danny just for the sake of marrying him." Laura paused. "Maybe we'll keep on seeing each other; and maybe after we both graduate, we'll have second thoughts about marriage, but not right now."

Mrs. Garza smiled. "I guess it does make sense. I can just hear what the neighbors will say. Then again we've always been a family that doesn't care about what the neighbors think," she said cheerfully as she patted Laura's hand in reassurance. She sighed in relief and remarked, "Well, I guess we've had our talk. What do you say we go get something to eat?"

"Now that you mention it, Mom, I am quite hungry," said Laura; and she stroked her tummy.

CHAPTER NINETEEN

*D*anny drove up his driveway with the radio at high volume, hoping it would block out the confusion in his mind. He wished, at least for a while, that he could forget that Laura was pregnant and that in less than five months he would be a daddy.

As he walked up to the mail box to get the mail, a letter regarding his S.A.T. scores arrived. Fear ran though his stomach. He walked into the house and sat down on the sofa. He opened the letter.

"What is it, sweetie?" asked Mrs. López.

Danny reluctantly answered, "Just my S.A.T. scores."

His mom's eyes lit up with excitement, "Just, just, S.A.T. scores? May I remind you that up until you found out Laura was pregnant, you couldn't wait for your results? Now, it's just S.A.T. scores. Are you all right? All you used to talked about were S.A.T. scores."

Danny half smiled.

"Well, open it, dear," continued his mom. She anxiously sat and waited.

"Somehow, it doesn't seem that exciting any more." He handed the letter to her.

"What? Son, what's wrong with you? Danny, it's not the end of the world," she tried to comfort him as best as possible. "Sweetheart, it breaks my heart to see you like this."

Danny felt her soft touch on his head. "Danny, we've talked with Laura's parents. We're going to help you out. Whatever your decision, we will stand by it.

Danny sat with his hands covering his forehead. "Mom, I don't know what to do. I feel I should stand by her. But I'm scared. I feel as if I'm being swallowed by confusion." As he talked, his voice began to shake.

"Oh, dear," she said with a smile on her face.

"I've ruined everything," he said.

"That's okay, son, cry. It's okay. It's okay to feel confused."

"Oh, look at me crying," he said. He quickly wiped his tears and tried to be strong. "Men don't cry."

"Whoever told you that, son?"

"Mom, don't you see? I have to be the strong one here."

"Now open the letter."

Danny opened the letter with no emotion. After finding out he'd soon be a daddy, nothing could make him feel better.

Mrs. López put her hands to her face. "Huh? What son? Tell me!"

Danny grinned. "What do you know? I scored extremely high."

Mrs. López leaned over to see his scores. She said cheerfully, "Danny, that's great. That's almost a perfect score." Her face lit up with delight. "Do you know what this means? You get to go to the college of your choice! Scholarships will be coming in left and right." She could barely control her emotions. "I'm calling your dad. You realize, Danny, this is the moment we've waited for all our lives," she continued as she cupped her hand to Danny cheeks. "We're so very proud of you, honey," she said.

"Ahh, come on, Ma." He put his arms around her. "It's not that big a deal. I've been thinking. Maybe I'll attend the local university here."

She pulled away from him and observed him with disbelief in her eyes. "What is it, Danny? Is it Laura? Is that what's getting you down? Well, it's her fault, that little tramp. She had no right to seduce you. You have to put all that behind you. Her parents will take care of her."

"Mom, you don't understand. I can't just keep ignoring her and pretend nothing happened. It's not all her fault. In fact, it's not her fault at all. I told her I'd be careful."

"No, sir. A woman has much more control over this situation than a man. She could have prevented it."

"Mom, I can't run away from it anymore. I have ignored Laura for too long. I've even considered going out with two other girls in hopes that I might forget about her," he said. He looked down and pounded the letter against his hand in a nervous manner. "I think, I think I'm going to ask Laura to marry me."

"Danny, son, please, think about this. It has only been a few days that you've known. We told you we'd help pay the bills for the baby."

"Mom, you don't understand. We could be apart for ten years, but I don't think I'd ever forget Laura and our baby. I'm a man with a conscience, and I can't do that. I'd never be able to forgive myself. Surely, you and Dad can understand that?"

She looked away from Danny. Tears ran down her face as she yelled, "So, this is it? Seventeen years down the drain? And what about us? Never mind that your father and I suffered and worked hard to get you everything you needed. This is the way you pay us back!" she yelled.

"Sorry, Mom, but I've made my decision. I'm not going away to a university. I must marry Laura and find a job while I attend the local university."

She continued yelling, "No, sir, I think we deserve a lot more than that! Your dad and I worked hard because we didn't have an education. But it will not happen to you. You will go away next year."

Danny had never felt so trapped in his entire life. He felt as if he'd fallen down a deep hole and would never be able to climb up to the surface. Danny turned and walked outside.

"Where are you going?"

"Ma, please, I have to leave."

The car brakes skidded loudly as he drove off. Julio heard the loud honk as Danny drove up his driveway. He ran out of the house.

"Danny, what's up? Want to go for a Coke?"

"Sure, why not?"

"What's up, Danny?"

"You want to go run a couple laps with me?"

Julio pushed his black curls from his forehead, "Hey, guy, we just finished practice. I need a break."

"Yeah, yeah, you're right," he said. He stopped the car by the track field.

"Hey, dude," he said with a puzzled look on his face. "What's up, Dan? What's really bothering you?"

Danny's mind was occupied. He was oblivious to Julio's words. "Julio, I don't know what I'm going to do about Laura's pregnancy."

"Oh, that, hey guy..." Julio said as he slapped Danny on his back.

"You already talked about that, didn't you? You said that you weren't going to marry her and that your parents were going to help out with the bills."

"I said that all right." He picked a rock to throw it as far as he could. "My parents made me say that, and I tried to believe it. That's not truly how I feel inside." He picked up another rock.

"Well, how do you feel?" asked Julio with a serious look on his face.

"I feel as if I'm responsible. And as bad as it may seem, I think it may turn out all right. I'm scared. Hell, I'm really scared. But I have to do what I have to do. I can't just leave her alone to face the consequences. Besides," he said shyly, "I still love her. I don't think I'll have feelings for anyone else ever again."

"If you feel that way about it, buddy, then do it. You know it's not going to be a bed of roses. Remember Maxine and Bob?"

"Who?" said Danny absentmindedly.

"Yeah, dude. They graduated last year."

"Oh, yeah?"

"Well, Maxine became pregnant right after graduation. They married, and I heard that they already separated."

"Yeah, dude. Well that will never happen to me," said Danny optimistically. "I think Laura and I can make it."

"I don't know, dude. You're going to have to get a part-time job. Laura will probably have to drop out of school. Worst of all, there will be baby crap everywhere. You'll no longer be the fun couple you were before."

"I have to do what I have to do, Julio, no matter what happens. If it doesn't work out, it doesn't work out."

Julio took a deep breath. "Dan, when do you intend to pop the question?" he asked with a frown.

Danny gave a yawn. "Listen, guy, it's kind of late. I think I'm going home and crash out early," said Danny. He yawned.

Julio put his hands in his pocket. "No problem, dude. I understand. You must have a million things on your mind."

Julio put his hand on Danny's shoulder and with a firm grip said, "If you ever need anything, Danny, you know, to talk about anything, give me a call, dude. See yah."

Danny arrived at his home. As he opened the front door, he found his dad sitting on the sofa smoking a pipe and reading the newspaper. Dan said the usual hello and proceeded to walk past him.

"Danny, I'm glad your home, son. Could you sit down for a while? I think we need to have a talk."

"Well, sure, Dad," he said as he flopped down on the sofa. He sat across from his dad, hoping his dad wouldn't notice his anxiety.

"Son," he said as he removed the pipe from his mouth, "your mother tells me you had an argument today. She feels bad about it."

"Yes, I do, Danny," said Mrs. López. She had appeared from the bedroom hall. "I am very sorry for what I said about Laura and everything else. I know you've been under a lot of stress lately." Tears began to roll down Mrs. López's face. "You think it doesn't hurt to see your little boy in trouble like this?"

"Mom, please, don't cry. I am not a little boy."

"Everything we worked so hard for—all our lives we put our dreams in you so that you could be something. We didn't have an education, and we had hopes and dreams that you would be different. But now these dreams are gone."

"Mom, it doesn't have to end that way. It's not over."

Mr. López gently took Mrs. López's hand, "Please settle down, honey."

Danny felt helpless and useless at the same time.

"Mom, please, don't cry. I wish this never would have happened."

Mr. López stood up from the sofa to comfort Mrs. López. Danny stood up from his seat in the hope that standing would make him feel more in control of himself.

"Anyway, what we were getting at, son," said Mr. López as he composed himself and cleared his throat, "what your mother and I are trying to tell you is that whatever your decision is, we will support it. If you and Laura don't get married, we will help support our grandchild until you can stand on your own two feet. If you do wish to marry, we will open our house to her, to you, and, of course, the baby. One thing we do ask is that you do not drop out of school, no matter what. Please, continue with your college education, no matter how difficult. We will pay for your tuition; only, please, let our dream be completed. That's all we ask."

Mrs. López stood looking down, not able to hold her head up. Tears continued to run down her face.

Danny felt an uncontrollable urge to cry. Tears filled his eyes. Since the time he was told by Laura of her pregnancy, he had not been able to let out the heavy burden he felt deep inside his heart. He walked toward his parents and embraced them both.

CHAPTER TWENTY

*L*aura walked through the entrance hall of San Manuel High. She stopped quickly as she felt the first signs of life moving inside of her.

"What is it, Laura?" asked Anna as she chewed the last piece of apple and flipped the core into the trash can.

"I...I... felt a flutter in my stomach. It must be the baby."

"Did you feel it move?" asked Anna secretly.

"Yes, I did," said Laura, still in doubt about whether to feel happy or ashamed.

"Well, this is my last exam," said Anna happily. "After this, Laura, my friend, we will be seniors. One more year until graduation." She pranced a few steps ahead of Laura. Laura's face lit up.

"Oh, my goodness," cried Anna.

"What is it?"

"Don't look now, but Prince Charming is coming."

"Hmmm...that's strange," thought Laura. To avoid a confrontation, for weeks Danny had avoided coming through this hall. Laura's heart raced. She walked to the other side of the crowded hall. She put her notebooks in front of her stomach to make sure no one would accidently bump into her. As she turned the combination on her locker, she felt someone grip her arm.

"Laura, Laura, may we talk?"

Laura's heart froze. She quickly recognized Danny's deep voice. Without turning to look at him, Laura said, "Danny, there's nothing to talk about. You're a jerk, a real big one."

"But I want to make it right between us. I miss you. I really miss you."

Laura turned and looked at Danny. She couldn't believe what she was hearing.

"I know finals are up."

"My last final is at 1:45. I know yours are too. May we talk after that?"

"Sure," said Laura.

Suddenly Danny took Laura's hand and kissed it. Laura was confused. She didn't know whether to slap him or hug him. In her confusion, she simply gave a half smile as he walked away.

The school year was coming to an end. This was the last exam. Laura sat and tried to concentrate on her exam; she found it difficult to keep Danny off her mind. She walked up to Mrs. Medrano's desk to turn in her test. Laura was in a daze while everyone was saying their good-byes. She was so engrossed by thoughts of Danny that she failed to see Thelma outside the classroom waiting for her.

"Laura," said Thelma, as she waved her hand in front of Laura's face.

"Are you all right? The test wasn't that hard, was it?"

"I don't think so," she continued sarcastically, "not

for—THELMA!" screamed Laura, finally noticing Thelma as she broke from her trance.

"Yes."

"You're back."

"Yes, I'm back. I took all my tests; and so far I believe I've aced them all, if I do say so myself," she said in a sassy manner.

"I'm so glad you came back to school, Thelma," said Laura. They simultaneously hugged each other in the middle of the hall.

"But, listen, Laura," said Thelma, as she grabbed Laura's hand, "I want to thank you a million times for going to talk to my dad about my not dropping out of school."

"Oh, that," said Laura absentmindedly.

"Yes, you and Mrs. Medrano went to talk to my dad. I don't know what Mrs. Medrano told my dad, but she hit it right on the button. Dad said that for this year we'll manage here in the valley. I'll work full time at the diner, and I believe we'll make it."

"Oh, Thelma, your dad is so sweet. There was nothing to it."

"He said that he saw you talking outside with my sister Myra and my brother Beto. Laura, he said he remembered when you and I were young and how we'd compete with each other for the highest grades in different subjects. Somehow, you made him realize all those rewards and studying must be worth something. He said he saw the deep concern in Mrs. Medrano's eyes."

Laura smiled. "Well, you earned it, Thelma. Now we'll be in competition for next year's highest ranking senior award."

"What are you talking about?" asked Thelma.

"You know, valedictorian," said Laura, with a smile, knowing deep inside that all her goals for such high achievements were of no use.

Laura moved her purse from one shoulder to the other. "Well, I'll see you soon, Thelma."

"I'll see you around. Come by the diner. I'll give you a free banana split, the kind you've been ordering a lot this year." Thelma waved good-bye.

"All right, thanks," said Laura as she waved good-bye.

CHAPTER TWENTY-ONE

*L*aura walked toward the girls' bathroom. She nervously searched her purse for her make-up and brush. "There," she thought. Her lipstick was intact; and her long, brown, silky hair seemed healthier than ever. It must have been the vitamins the doctor prescribed for her and the baby. "Well, Laura," she said to herself, "this is it. You and Dan are finally going to talk. You're not going to fall apart as you did last time." She took a deep breath and walked to her locker. Turning the corner to the hall, she could see Danny standing and waiting by the locker door. Danny turned, and their eyes met.

"Hi, Laura. Hello again. I am so glad you could make it."

"Yeah, well, I guess we do need to talk," she said tossing her hair over her shoulder.

"Would you like to go some place else to talk?" he asked.

"Well, whatever. It doesn't matter," said Laura proudly. She was beginning to feel the first symptoms of anger and betrayal rush through her heart.

"Why don't we talk now? Let's just get it over with," she said.

Danny's heart raced to his throat. He tried to relax and find the words. "Please, Laura, I know I've been a total jerk."

"That's putting it mildly," said Laura, pretending to act boldly. She dialed the combination to the locker.

Danny was at a loss for words. He reached over and gently touched Laura's shoulder. Laura suddenly jerked back, and Danny's hand retracted quickly.

"Laura, will you just listen, please?"

Laura turned to him, drew a deep breath, crossed her arms, and put her head down.

"I know you're going through a major change in your life."

"Ha, yeah, you could say that!"

"Shh...shh...let me finish. I'm going through a major change in my life, too. You're going to have to live with your decision for the rest of your life, and so am I. I avoided you for a long time because I was scared and didn't or wouldn't deal with the problem."

"Yeah, well, how do you think I was feeling with my belly growing before my eyes and my body going berserk?"

Danny cupped his hand over Laura's mouth.

"Shhh...shhh...there still are students in the hall."

"I don't care," said Laura. She wiped the tears from her face.

"Please, Laura. Let's go somewhere else and talk. How about Ginger Park?" Laura nodded silently in approval.

The drive to the park was a silent one. When Danny parked the car, Laura opened the door on her side.

"Wait, wait," said Danny as he hurriedly rushed to her side to help her open the door.

"Danny, I'm pregnant, not crippled," she said with a grin on her face.

"Well," he said as he grabbed her hand to help her out, "I think it would be nice to pamper you for a change. I might as well start."

Laura was bewildered by his actions. They walked and finally chose a picnic table in order to sit down to sort out their problems. They both were silent for a minute and at exactly the same time decided to speak.

"Danny..."

"Laura. Whoops. You were going to speak. Go ahead."

"No, you first," said Laura.

"You sure?"

"Yes, I'm sure."

"Laura," said Danny, looking into her eyes. "I've been pretty stupid for ignoring you. I was scared and confused. I didn't want to think about you. I really didn't want to accept it. But I can't get you out of my mind. I think about you, and I want to pick up the phone and call you. But then I remember that you are pregnant, and I get scared. I don't know what happened to me. I love you, and that baby is mine. I want to accept responsibility for it. I'm ready, Laura."

Laura tried hard to keep tears from rolling down her face. She didn't want Danny to think she was a weak woman.

"Laura, this decision will change my life forever. I'm scared; but I feel that with God on our side and our love for each other, we will make it through."

He gently put his hand in hers. "Laura, I know that Saint Jude's University isn't the college we would like to attend. But, it's not really that bad. We could live with my parents. I could work part time. Meanwhile, I'm sure your parents, as well as mine, would agree to help us out with the baby. We could get a sitter, Laura. What I'm trying to say is, will you marry me?"

While Laura's mind was racing with thoughts of distrust and pain, her eyes were filled with anger and fear. Yet her heart and soul were secure and peaceful. Danny had finally come to his senses. That's all she wanted to hear. That's all she wanted to know. Without a word, Danny and Laura embraced for a long while. Her arms were wrapped around his shoulders; his encircled her waist. Danny remained calm; he tried to make her feel calm. Laura tried to stop crying in order to tell Danny what she really wanted from this serious situation that faced them.

Laura pulled her face from his chest. She looked at Danny. "Please don't get upset at what I'm going to say." She took a deep breath. "Danny, I think it would be a big mistake if we married now."

Danny looked confused. "I don't know about that, Laura."

"What's not to know?" she went on. Danny lifted her onto the picnic table. "We'll still date. You can see the baby anytime you want, and you and I won't feel trapped. You'll get a scholarship to D.L.C. University and visit the baby and me on holidays. I will attend Saint Jude's University. When we're ready to commit to one another, we will."

"Laura, I am ready to commit to you right now. Let's

just get married."

"Danny," Laura said raising her voice loudly, "you are missing the larger picture. I know you are ready, but maybe I'm not. I feel boxed in enough as it is. I don't want to be one of those girls that gets married and divorced all in the same year."

Danny looked lovingly into Laura's eyes, knowing well that his words and choices were second to Laura's. "Laura, in your life, you're only going to feel one pair of lips kiss you," said Danny before he kissed Laura.

After they kissed, Laura said, "Danny, please, please don't force me. The only people that will gossip will be the neighbors and some schoolmates. You know as well as I do that rumors only go as far as when the next one starts. I don't care what people say. I only know what I feel in my heart. I know I can't speak for all the girls in my position. Each one of us is different and makes our own choices according to who we are and our beliefs. So, now," she continued, "I've made another choice. It doesn't mean I don't love you. No matter what comes between us, I'll always love you," she said softly. "You were my first love."

"Hey," said Danny, jokingly but nervous, "I'll be your only love."

"What a tough position you have, Danny. I really didn't think about it until now. I'm so happy about your decision to ask me to marry you. Until a few minutes ago, I really wasn't sure where you truly stood."

"I am so sorry," said Danny.

"But now we must be really serious about this matter, Danny," she continued. She pulled away from his embrace. "I've been thinking a lot about this, as well. I've discussed this with my mother. Danny, please, don't fight me on this. I know in my heart this is the best thing to do because I love you, and I know you love me. This is the best decision to ensure that if later we still feel the same way about each other, we'll be able to marry happily."

"Laura, I don't understand you."

Laura trembled and nervously rubbed her arm. "Danny, we can't get married, not now, not next year."

"But I love you."

"I know. I know. I love you, too. It's just not the smart way out." Laura paused for a while. "We're both mature people. Danny, these last few months have made me mature so much more. I've become extremely realistic about the situation. I've thought the decision through in my mind, over and over again."

Tears began rolling down Laura's face. She wiped them nonchalantly. She'd become used to crying.

"We have parents who will help us out for a few years. I can stay and take care of the baby. I've already talked to Mr. Salinas in confidence." She continued, "For the month I'll miss school, I'll take correspondence courses. I can still graduate with the class. Please, Danny," she said, "please understand me."

Danny stepped back. He took a deep breath and reluctantly said, "We'll try it your way for a while. If problems begin, then we'll do it my way. Is that fair enough?"

"Fair enough," said Laura with a smile. Her lips quickly met his. All was understood. "Thank you for understanding, Danny."

CHAPTER TWENTY-TWO

*I*t was one year after high school graduation. Laura walked into her bedroom and softly laid baby Daniel in the crib. He moved restlessly. Laura tenderly lulled him to sleep. "Hush, pumpkin. I have to get dressed to go out with your dad tonight," she said, slowly moving away from the crib. She bumped into the lamp table and accidently knocked over a senior prom picture of her and Danny on the floor. She picked up the picture. She smiled joyously as she embraced the picture close to her heart. Somehow, she knew she would cherish this picture forever.

Laura shut her eyes and envisioned how beautifully decorated the Civic Center looked. She remembered its immense, silver, glass chandeliers hanging from the ceiling. The streamers, balloons, and cotton-made clouds fit the theme "Stairway to Heaven." She had chosen an off-the-shoulder, royal-blue evening gown which was fitted at the waist with an oversized bow at the back. A mix of light blue carnations and baby's breath around her wrist added the perfect touch. Danny stood pridefully by her with a black tuxedo and royal-blue cummerbund. He had a light royal-blue carnation pinned to his tuxedo. She laughed loudly, as she gazed down at the high-top, black tennis shoes Danny and "the gang" decided to wear—a touch of class, they insisted. It had been a great evening.

Laura gently put the framed picture back on the lamp

table and walked to her dresser. There was a gold picture frame of Anna. It took her back to another glorious moment. A warm, pleasant feeling ran through Laura's body. Goose bumps rose on her arms as she remembered the glorious event. Her best friend received a wonderful surprise. She was named homecoming queen of San Manuel High. "How very proud I was of you, as I waited anxiously by the field waiting for your coronation to be over. I could hardly wait to hug you," Laura thought. Tears ran from her eyes, but this time they were happy tears. Anna's photogenic smile and 12-inch rhinestone crown looked spectacular. Even though the camera was in front of her, Anna's eyes looked up to the sky. "What was it, Anna?" thought Laura. "Did you feel your sister watching you from heaven? Thank you, Anna, for being a great friend to me during and after my pregnancy. Months went by, and you kept my secret. I know we were both relieved when it was finally over." Laura's secret was now out, a beautiful, handsome baby boy.

Laura gazed at baby Daniel. Then she picked up the group graduation photo of her and all her friends. She wiped the dust from the frame and whispered, "Yes, Thelma, you earned it. You worked hard to win the title of valedictorian and a full, four-year scholarship to Harvard University. Your parents were elated, to say the very least." Laura once again closed her eyes for a moment and remembered the proud faces of Mr. and Mrs. Muñoz. Money was earned and spent, but an educated son or daughter brought pride, joy, and a guarantee that their child would not experience as hard a life as they had endured.

"My only regret is that I wasn't able to compete

against you our senior year. Maybe I would have been valedictorian." Sadness came over Laura as she said the words. She felt as if a volcano was erupting inside her soul. She squeezed her eyes shut and took a deep breath. "Oh, well," she thought. "It was my mistake, my choice, and my life. Everything turned out for the best, considering the circumstances." Laura ran her fingers through her hair as she put the picture back and gave a heavy sigh.

She turned to the portrait of Danny and her in their graduation gowns. Danny had also won a scholarship. He had worked hard to earn his scholarship. She walked calmly back to the window and peeked through the curtain. The sun was going down. It would soon be dark. She could still see some of the remains of the party—pieces of the piñata scattered about as well as candy wrappers from her son's first birthday party. "Yes," she thought as she folded her arms in front of her. "I had to grow up really fast. I was able to enter Saint Jude's University." She thought of how fortunate she was that her mom and dad were able to afford a baby sitter for their first grandchild. Had it not been for that, it would have been almost impossible to continue school. Her daddy had refused to let her work until she graduated from the university. She knew of other girls in her school who faced the same dilemma but had to drop out of school to work. Another choice had been to give her baby up for adoption. Still another choice was to terminate her pregnancy by the first trimester. Laura thought of how very supportive Danny's parents had been.

She threw herself on the bed and reminisced about the year that had passed so quickly. She gave an exhausted sigh. She thought of all the new friends she met this year as a beginning freshman at the local university. She thought of the countless parties she'd already been invited to but had disregarded. She still felt somewhat uncomfortable about attending parties, knowing at home in her bedroom was a crib with a baby boy who was her responsibility.

She placed her left hand in front of her face and admired the beautiful 1/2-carat, marquise, diamond ring given to her by Danny. Yes, plans had changed. Laura and Danny agreed that being apart wasn't the best for the baby or them. They would be married toward the end of spring semester. Danny decided he would make the move and transfer to the local university with Laura. Laura felt content and ready for that move. In a way, it was good that she and Danny had not been with each other constantly. This past year she needed the distance and the time to sort out the tangled web she felt she'd fallen into. She was now ready to proceed with her life and so was Danny. In the meantime, he insisted on getting a part-time job to be able to help her parents with the bills.

It was Thanksgiving weekend. The entire gang had made a point to come down from all the different universities to help Laura and Danny celebrate the baby's first birthday. A soft knock on the door brought Laura out of her deep thoughts.

"Yes, Mom?"

"Sweetie, Danny is here to pick you up."

Laura jumped from her bed and looked at her clock. It was 8:30 already. "Oh, my God! Tell him I'll be right out, Mom."

Laura hurriedly retouched her make-up and changed her clothes. She wore a shapely, bright red dress which reached the top of her knees. "This will grab Danny's attention. I won't be seeing him for another three weeks," she thought. She bought the dress on sale and had saved it for a special occasion. She ran her fingers through her hair and finished applying her red lipstick.

"May I come in?" a deep, male voice asked.

"Come in, Danny."

"How is my junior?"

"He is doing great," said Laura. " You just saw him, silly." Danny's eyes grew wide when he saw Laura's curvy body bring the red dress to life. "You are so sexy and thin. I think you lost even more weight."

"Oh, Danny."

"Are you eating?"

"Yes, of course, I am. It's just that I have so many other things to do. Besides, I'm only two pounds less than I weighed before I became pregnant. You are just used to seeing me chubby."

"Well, anyway..." He grabbed her waist and drew her toward him.

"You are so beautiful."

Laura embraced him lovingly. Danny felt Laura's closeness, and a passionate kiss reminded them of their never-ending love.

"Knock, knock, may I come in?"

"Sure, Mom."

Laura pulled away from Danny's arms, still feeling the embarrassment of being caught kissing.

"Mom, where's Gloria?" she asked as she retouched the lipstick on her mouth.

"She's washing clothes. But, don't worry. The baby will be fine. He's sleeping now. He's had a long day."

Danny walked over to the crib. "Hey, son," he said lovingly as he put his hand on the baby's forehead. "You're gonna be all right. Soon we'll be together, and you'll be just fine. You hear that, son." Danny, Jr. slept peacefully in his crib. He had inherited his dad's deep, dark eyebrows and long, curly eyelashes. His jet black hair also matched Danny's hair. Laura slowly crept to Danny's side and took his hand. She felt his fingers lacing themselves through her own. They both stood in silence and watched the baby sleeping.

Danny turned to Laura. "I'll return back to the university early tomorrow morning, Laura. I won't see you and the baby until Christmas."

Laura felt an emptiness run through her. She raised her hand to Danny's lips and whispered, "Let's not think about it right now, Danny." She quieted him by bringing her lips to his. A sweet feeling of surrender came over Danny.

They welcomed the feeling and love that ran through their bodies. Laura gently pushed away. "Anna and the rest of the clan said they'd meet us at the club. We'd better take off.

Chapter Twenty-Two

We don't want to be late."

"You're right. We'd better leave before I won't be able to stop myself again. We won't go anywhere for the rest of the night—like last night."

Laura blushed at the thought of last night's love. She knew that even though her thoughts were clear and she was ready to marry Danny that moment, it would be more important to sacrifice themselves now. Let them both get as many college hours as possible before getting married.

CHAPTER TWENTY-THREE

The dance hall roared with good times, with lively dancing music. When Laura and Danny walked into the nightclub, Anna and Kevin signaled them from across the dance floor.

"Danny, they're over there!" screamed Laura, hoping her voice could be heard over the music.

Laura's red dress turned heads. She wore her hair down, tossed over to one side of her shoulder. Danny wore jeans and a long-sleeve, white shirt. Working out and lifting weights had changed Danny. Female heads turned as he walked by. Laura was aware of this. He wasn't the tall, lanky high school basketball player any longer. He'd matured into a much more sophisticated and substantial man. She felt a placid pride in knowing he belonged to her, heart and soul.

"Hi, everybody!" shouted Laura. She waved across the table then sat down with her friends. They exchanged kisses even though they'd just seen each other at Danny, Jr.'s party.

"That was a neat birthday party, Danny," yelled Kevin. "Jr.'s a big boy, a big one year old." Kevin, Ricky, Thelma, Julio, Danny, Marcy, and Anna were all together again. They laughed and reminisced about their high school years. They all took turns dancing with each other. When the song "True Friends Will Be Friends Forever" began to play, the entire group stepped onto the dance floor and formed a circle.

Each took a turn dancing in the middle of their circle of friends. They had often done that when they went out to clubs. As they danced, Danny felt a strong bond with his friends, a deep sense of loyalty. He could not describe it. He only knew that if he had the chance to trade the feeling for a million dollars, he would never do it.

Julio walked over to Laura. "Laura, want to dance?"

"Why, of course," she replied. She joined Julio near the dance floor. Danny wasn't much of a dancer, so she was glad Julio had asked her.

"Dance with her as much as you can, Valentino. Soon she will be my bride. Then hands off!" Julio and Daniel slapped high fives. Then Laura led Julio onto the floor.

It seemed that the night would never end. But before anyone knew it, it was 2 a.m. and time to leave the club. As the clan walked out of the club, Ricky yelled, "The night is still young! Who knows when we'll all be together again. Let's take it to Pepe's. It's open all night. Let's go have breakfast."

"That's a great idea," affirmed Marcy. She'd gained some weight during her one year of college. But no one seemed to notice. Her body may have changed, but her heart was as warm as ever.

"Yeah!" cried Kevin. "Who knows? The next time we meet, someone may already be married or fall in love and prefer to be with their love, alone."

Julio looked over at Laura and Danny, "You guys aren't going to be party poopers, are you?"

Laura felt guilty. She knew she should be home with Danny, Jr.; but this was so tempting, and they were right. Who knew when they would meet again? The last few times they had tried to meet, their plans fell through. This was the first time since graduation night that they all had managed to come together. All of them had reorganized their work schedules just to be able to be here for baby Daniel's birthday party. Danny and Laura grinned at each other.

"Why not?" replied Danny. "We'll just call home and make sure everything is all right."

"Great. Let's go!" yelled Anna.

The aroma of scrumptious, hot french fries; juicy burgers; and spicy onion rings filled the restaurant. The waitress designated a table for the group. Julio seemed to be the only one listening to the waitress. As Julio and Rick made their way to the table, Rick was stopped by countless friends. The restaurant seemed to belong to all of them.

Laura was at one end of the restaurant talking to friends while Danny was at the opposite side showing pictures of Danny, Jr. He boasted how much he looked like him. "Se mira igual que yo. Don't you think so?" His friends shook his hand and patted him on the back.

Anna was hugging friends. Kevin had gone to the restroom, and Marcy was in the powder room. Eventually, they all made their way back to the table.

Everyone was talking at the same time. They tried to catch up on everything that they'd done in the last year. The guys talked about everything—weights, girls, boots, drinks, gum, and college courses. The girls talked about make-up, new boyfriends or dates, diets, classes, and intended majors.

Anna took a fork and gently tapped it against a glass. "Attention, everyone." When she had the full attention of everyone, she announced, "I have decided what my degree will be." She put the fork down and crossed her hands.

"Oh, really, Miss Homecoming Queen," coaxed Marcy. "What, may I ask, would that be?"

"Well, you know I've always loved audiences. I just can't see any of that coming to an end. I'm taking my basics here. Then the world better get ready because I'm going to Hollywood. I will make it to the big movie screen," she said happily.

Laura's mouth fell open.

"Are you surprised, Laura?"

"Extremely." Laura swallowed. She thought she would choke. She coughed loudly from the surprising and wonderful news.

Ricky was sitting next to Laura. He gave her a slap on her back. "Are you all right?"

"Yes," gasped Laura. "Anna, when did you decide? When we were little girls, Thelma, you, and I pretended to be singers. I thought, maybe, you'd be a singer."

"The large trophies and constant honors announced over the intercom by our principal weren't clues, Laura?"

Laura tossed her hair over her shoulder. "How many people win trophies in something but never pursue a career in that area? How many football players go on to pro football? How many cheerleaders decide to go on to be cheerleaders at universities? Anna, I'm so elated for you."

"I can't stand this wonderful news," Julio blurted out.

"We'll be watching you, girl," said Rick.

Anna smiled serenely. "Thanks, guys. You're the best." Anna's voice trembled. "Thelma, Laura, you guys were like my sisters. I don't think I could have made it through the death of my sister if you girls hadn't been there for me. I owe a lot to both of you."

Laura's almond-shaped, brown eyes sparkled with laughter. "That's so sweet."

Thelma coughed nervously, remembering the tragic death. "Yeah, Anna, that's very sweet. It was a pleasure standing by you," said Thelma.

Kevin leaned over and said to Anna, "Hey, baby, you can be my actress any day."

Anna grabbed Kevin's arm lovingly and squeezed it.

"Huh..." Thelma cleared her throat. Everyone's head turned to her. She moved her chair closer to the table. "Well, now that the subject has been brought up, I made a decision too."

Danny raised his hand and interrupted, "Wait, don't tell me. Let me guess." Thelma flashed a smile. Her hazel eyes lit up her face. "You want to be a surgeon?"

She took a swipe at Danny. "No, I don't."

"You want to be a brain surgeon?" He continued the teasing.

"No."

"Well, tell us," said Julio.

"Well, I've always had an interest in it. I'm going to get my B.A. in pre-law and then...."

Laura stopped Thelma and asked, "You're going to law school?"

"Right on, the money, buddy," said Thelma pleased.

"I knew it! I knew it! Your quest for knowledge and answers to rules which seemed wrong to you were big clues." Marcy ran her hair through her fingers, "Well, I know whom I'll be going to for representation or when I need a job as an executive secretary."

Kevin leaned forward, "Is that what you want to be, Marcy?"

"Yeah. I know it's not as prestigious as all of you, but I really like it. I think I'll truly be happy doing that."

Danny put his arm around Laura, "Hey, happiness is what's important."

Julio set his chin on his fist and leaned on the table, "Okay, okay. Let's not get mushy."

"What about you, Mr. Muscle Man?"

Julio rolled up his shirt and flaunted his muscles. They were a sight to see.

Chapter Twenty-Three

Rick put his hand over his face. "Este dude, what a show-off, man."

"Yeah, well, if you have it, flaunt it."

"Hey, stud, why don't you flaunt yourself and catch our waitress' eye. I'm ready for another drink and some food."

"Yes, are you all ready to order?" Julio took control. "How many Cokes?"

"I want one," said Laura.

"Okay, okay, let's do this in an orderly manner," said Julio jokingly.

"Raise your hands, children, for those who want Coke."

"That will be six Cokes, two Sprites, eight cheeseburgers, and eight orders of french fries."

"I don't want any onions on my burger," Laura jumped in.

"I don't either," replied Marcy.

"Ditto that," said Anna.

"Okay, I have your order. It should be ready in about twenty minutes. I'll bring your drinks first," the waitress said. She put the order slip in her pocket and walked away.

"So, Julio, what were you saying, before you rudely interrupted yourself?"

Julio put his hands together and raised his left eyebrow, acting seriously. "I think I'd love to get into business eventually. My dad taught me about the growing economy here in South Texas. We could very well become a world trade center.

I'm going to get a degree in business. I like the import/export areas."

Danny took his arm from around Laura's shoulder.

Julio mischievously took a straw that was still in its wrapper, cut one end of it with his teeth, and blew into the straw. The paper wrapper flew off.

"So, what about you, Daniel?"

"I believe engineering would suit me well. I'll begin my courses as soon as I transfer to the university."

Laura lowered her face, fearing it would be her turn. She would have liked to be like all the others. Because she became pregnant, she was not able to go to the university of her choice and receive her degree as a pediatrician. She would have to settle for the highest degree in nursing she could get at Saint Jude's University, the local college. She had thought of transferring, but the burden would be too great. She could only hope for an extension medical program to open at St. Jude's. Rumors of that were stirring.

Laura reminded herself how lucky she was to have been raised in a middle-income family. Thanks to her parents, she at least had the opportunity to pursue her nursing degree.

Anna waved her hand in front of Laura's face. "Hello. Earth to Mars?"

Laura smiled. She looked at Thelma and Anna. She had often told them what she wanted to be and how she was going to do it. They already knew what career she preferred and also what she would have to settle for.

Thelma interrupted before Laura could speak. "Let me guess, you want to become a registered nurse?"

Laura smiled, "Yes, I do. I will have my degree in two years, Anna. Maybe even sooner."

Laura looked up.

"Heads up," said the waitress. She carried a large tray filled with their orders. "Okay, cheeseburger, no onions," she began.

Anna took a napkin and took the gum out of her mouth and wrapped it inside the napkin. "That's my burger."

They passed the different orders and drinks to each other. Thelma took a sip of her soft drink, "Don't think we forgot you, Rick."

Rick put a french fry into his mouth, "What?"

"It's your turn to tell us what you hope to do."

Rick cleared his throat, "Yeah, well..."

Kevin interrupted, "Pass the ketchup."

"Be quiet, Kevin. Let's hear Rick," said Thelma.

"Yeah, yeah, well, since I've always loved to draw, I've decided..."

Danny looked at Rick, "You want to be an artist!"

"Hey, you're not getting funny on me, are you, dude?" asked Kevin.

"Shut up, man. Let me finish. I figure I'll get a degree at Pan American in architecture. Since you people are all claiming to be so rich, I'll build all your homes, and your friends' homes, and your friends' friends' homes."

Laura looked over at Kevin, "Kevin, what about you?"

"I already said it."

"No, you didn't."

"You guys know I love agriculture."

Laura wiped her mouth with a napkin, "Well, yes, we know, but what degree?"

"I don't know, some sort of degree in agriculture. I'll figure it out when I get there."

They finished their cheeseburgers and fries and sat slurping their soft drinks. Rick ordered a last round. When the waitress brought it to the table, Rick took his spoon and hit it up against his glass.

"Okay, what now?" mumbled Daniel.

"I'd like to make a toast, a toast to great, everlasting friends. Tomorrow, we'll all go our separate ways. Who knows when we'll all be together again?"

Silence hung around the table. Everyone toasted one another. Smiles flashed as feelings of warmth and deep loyalty filled them. Some may never fulfill their desires and career goals, but it didn't matter. Respect for one another would always be there. They all knew that whatever the future held for them, no matter how many separations there would be, they would always remain in the center of each other's hearts and thoughts.